Fresh Roses

Fresh Roses

Teachers as Newcomers: Learning the Ropes at a New School

A Naturalistic Novel

Reva Chatman-Buckley

Major Professor for the research project:
Dr. Terrence E. Deal, former professor at George
Peabody College of Vanderbilt University

authorHOUSE®

AuthorHouse™
1663 Liberty Drive
Bloomington, IN 47403
www.authorhouse.com
Phone: 1 (800) 839-8640

Published by AuthorHouse 01/05/2016

ISBN: 978-1-5049-6107-3 (sc)
ISBN: 978-1-5049-6106-6 (e)

Library of Congress Control Number: 2015918596

Print information available on the last page.

Any people depicted in stock imagery provided by Thinkstock are models, and such images are being used for illustrative purposes only. Certain stock imagery © Thinkstock.

This book is printed on acid-free paper.

ABOUT THE AUTHOR

Reva Chatman-Buckley is an associate professor in the College of Education at Lipscomb University. She joined the faculty at Lipscomb University in 2009, after having served as a supervisor of student teachers. Prior to joining the faculty at Lipscomb University, she served as an adjunct professor at Tennessee State University and a charter school principal at a local middle school. She has spent 32 years in public education as an English teacher, assistant principal, curriculum principal, coordinator of student disciplinary referrals, and director of human resources.

She earned both her B.S. and M. Ed. degrees in English from Tennessee State University, where she minored in administration and supervision. In 1992, she earned her doctorate in educational leadership from George Peabody College of Vanderbilt University. While at Vanderbilt, she was nominated Graduate Researcher of the Year for her research surrounding teachers as newcomers. Her article titled *"Learning the Ropes Alone"* appeared in the spring, 1989 publication of *Action in Teacher Education*, the journal of the Association of Teacher Education. This article was co-authored by the renowned, Dr. Terence E. Deal, who served as her major professor while at Vanderbilt.

Fresh Roses was first accepted for publication back in 1995, but the contract ended rather abruptly when she refused to change the gender of the male teacher who was modeling best practices. Disappointed, she postponed seeking other publishers after her husband died of lung cancer and she unexpectedly became the legal guardian of her sister's four teenagers. She is convinced, however, that *Fresh Roses* is just as relevant today as it was twenty years ago, as little has changed in terms of the induction, orientation and socialization of new teachers. *Fresh Roses* should be of interest to all colleges of education, teacher education program leaders, pre-service educators, superintendents, principals, student teachers, new teachers and experienced teachers.

"The Purple Rose" poem by Dan Dammann

CONTENTS

ACKNOWLEDGMENTS

The completion of this book would not have been possible without the many personal sacrifices made by my deceased husband, Walter Chatman, my current husband, Bill and my mother, Allie. They served as my invincible cheering squad, for which I am eternally grateful. When I lost the electronic version of this manuscript, my sister, Melba, painstakingly re-typed the manuscript in its entirety. I am most grateful for her willingness to embrace such a challenge.

The six participants in this study gave of their time freely and allowed me to further disrupt a world already filled with spurts of disruption and chaos. I sincerely appreciate their indulgence.

Terry Deal, my mentor and major professor, envisioned that this project was possible for me long before I dared to dream of such a possibility. I owe him a debt of gratitude for believing in me when I did not believe in myself.

To the wonderful writer who read my first feeble attempts to frame this novel, Phyllis Gobell, I will be forever grateful. Without her encouragement, this first novel would have been abandoned long before its impetus. She is a master of gentle, constructive criticism.

Several special friends deserve mention because they served as constant sources of support. They are Commissioner Candice McQueen, Minnie Buchanan, Dan Dammann, and Jeanne Fain.

DEDICATION

To new, veteran, and aspiring teachers.

FOREWORD

Each year, universities grant hundreds of doctoral degrees to graduate students who have completed the demanding requirements. The final requisite is often a five chapter dissertation, a piece of original research dealing with some sort of significant problem. After hundreds of hours of working primarily with a major professor, a draft is defended in front of select faculty. For the most part, the staccato questions and penetrating bouts of the ancient ritual end on a positive note. The graduate student is welcomed to the academic or professional elite: a Doctor of Philosophy or of a specific profession (Education or Business).

But what happens to the dissertation? It is almost always a large tome representing hours of mind-numbing and thought-provoking toil. It is catalogued, copies given to key people, especially the student's advisor and core committee. It may be browsed by close members of the family, typically with great pride but little joy. It will sometimes be cited by others in their dissertation's bibliography. But rarely will significant findings of a thesis be applied to enlighten a problem it set out to explore.

Reva Chatman-Buckley's thesis you are about to read is a delightful departure from the norm. In terms of a defined problem, a relevant bibliography and a well thought out qualitative methodology, Reva's thesis follows conventional rules. Her in-depth studies of six new teachers entering the profession tease out some fundamental issues as the rookies encounter the ropes to skip and the ropes to know. Her findings support a major problem in American education. New idealistic teachers, entering the profession and assuming control of their first classroom, hit a wall. For many, it's sink or swim. Little help from colleagues; fresh meat for students. As a result, they leave.

Reva chose to present her findings through a novel, interweaving the actual experiences of new teachers in her research with a dramatic imaginary depiction... a story. The story focuses on Gail Simmons and how her experiences, unlike those of some of her novice colleagues, led to her early departure from the classroom. The dialogue will make you laugh, and cry. But it is a colorful depiction of what happens to hundreds of new teachers who enter and leave the profession each year.

Fresh Roses should be read by every new teacher entering the profession as well as those old-timers and school principals who can either make the going smoother or let the newcomers fend for themselves.

Here, finally, a dissertation with an afterlife. And my highest respect to someone with enough hutzpah to make it happen. Reva, you have my utmost admiration. It was a joy working with you.

Terrence E. Deal

INTRODUCTION

This novel had its genesis during my childhood. When I was a child I questioned everything. My favorite question was why. Once I knew why, I wanted to know how. Although I was chastised by my parents and ridiculed by my brothers and sisters, the questions never ceased. I possessed an insatiable desire to know and understand my world, yet I was much too young to realize its' complexity.

My growing knowledge of the world's complexity did not lessen my curiosity. I learned to pose questions with a higher degree of sophistication, but they were questions none the less. Many times my classmates would invite me to ask the questions they were afraid to pose. Teachers tolerated my questions, however; for I made certain that I answered as many as I asked.

By the time I graduated from high school it was common knowledge that I intended to become a news reporter or writer, commissioned to ask questions and disclose answers to life's dilemmas. As I applied to one college after another, I made it emphatically clear that journalism was my primary interest. As the dates for college entrance grew closer, however, my parents revealed that they could not afford to send me to the college of my choice. The scholarship that I had been awarded would cover tuition for a local university, but there was no money to pay for travel expenses or out-of-state fees. My hopes were dashed when I was forced to enroll in a university which did not offer journalism as a major field of study. My disappointment was even more pronounced when I learned that the university offered only one course in journalism.

"The closest thing we have to journalism is English," my college advisor stated. "A strong background in English will be exactly what you need to prepare you for a career in journalism." I reluctantly followed his advice and majored in English.

Many of us who were college students in the sixties were admonished to get certified to teach in case we could not reach our primary goals, so I took this advice as well. Four years later I found myself reporting to the local school board for an interview.

I remember reporting to the personnel office at 8:00 a.m. one crisp October morning, signing the teaching contract, and being told to report directly to Watson Middle School. I was excited to become a teacher! It was not journalism, but it was a respectable job.

My high school English teacher, Mrs. Burrows, had provided the perfect model for teaching. She was terrific. I shall never forget how carefully she formed her letters when she wrote on the chalkboard and how fluently she spoke. I was determined to be just like her.

I had no idea where Watson Middle School was located, so I followed the map very carefully. I shall never forget how the school looked. It was a rambling building with hundreds of windows and many more classrooms than my alma mater contained. As I parked my car and walked toward that red brick building at approximately 10:00 a.m., it never occurred to me that I would be facing my very own class of thirty students at 10:05.

When I walked into the principal's office to introduce myself, he remarked that I looked no older than his teenage daughter. He then asked me to follow him down to Room 110. On the way, he paused long enough to ask me where I was from and if I were married. This exchange took only two minutes.

At 10:02 he was introducing me to the substitute teacher whom he said needed to leave in order to report to another school. The substitute hurriedly showed me the roll book, pointed out a few topics the students had covered since the beginning of school and apologized for the mountain of ungraded papers stacked on the edge of her desk. I waited for more information, but none was offered. She left and I never heard from her again. I looked around for the principal but he, too, had vanished into oblivion.

The students and I stared at one another for what seemed an eternity. Realizing that my legs were weakening, I hurriedly sat on the edge of the chair situated behind the antiquated, battered desk. I felt frightened and confused, but I was thankful for the familiar desk which served as my refuge. Then a student arose and brought an assignment to the desk. This precipitated a steady stream of papers handed in by students who paused long enough to get a closer look at this newcomer. One student finally posed a question.

"Are you the real teacher or just a substitute?" she asked. When I assured her that I was the real teacher, she smiled and proceeded back to her desk. She paused along the way just long enough to tell each student in her row that I was the real teacher. I watched that whole row of smiling faces and could not help but smile back. This warm exchange gave me the courage to rise from my desk and move toward the chalkboard.

A piece of chalk lay in one corner of the board and an eraser in the other. The chalk which I clutched tightly in my hand felt familiar, as if it belonged there. I very carefully wrote my name across the board and felt confident enough to turn around and speak to the class. I do not remember my exact words, but I do remember that I somehow managed to make it through that day knowing that the students were glad I was there.

At the end of that day, I decided to walk to the room next door to meet one of my colleagues. She was a very tall, stately lady, much older than myself. After I introduced myself, she took one look at me and remarked, "I know you're not old enough to teach."

"Yes," I responded rather optimistically, "I was hired just this morning!"

"Well," she sighed, "I wish you luck, but you're mighty young to have to deal with this crowd. They have had four substitutes since the beginning of school. You're really going to have to be tough." She motioned for me to move out into the hallway so she could lock her door.

"Do you have any advice for me?" I asked.

"Yes," she said, "don't smile until Christmas! A new teacher should never smile for the first six weeks." Having said that, she walked down the long hallway toward the parking lot.

I went back to my room and straightened the long rows of student desks. As I picked up the stack of ungraded papers and turned to close the door, I suddenly thought, "Gee, I've already broken the first rule!"

It was against this backdrop that my teaching career began and that this study evolved. Like so many teachers in classrooms across the United States, I managed to somehow learn the ropes. How I learned the ropes and gained the knowledge and skills necessary to become a successful member of Watson Middle School, however, remain unclear. There are times when I am convinced I learned the ropes by trial and error. That is, like a scientist, I experimented with various approaches and tested a number of strategies until I finally selected the approach that worked best at Watson Middle.

Then there are times when the process seems to have been intuitive. These are the occasions when I just seemed to know, automatically, what to do and how to do it as if I had been programmed. Finally, there are the times when I remember having gone directly to someone in the organization to ask exactly how something was to be done.

My first day in Room 110 at Watson Middle School was unsettling. But when did things begin to take shape? How did I learn the beliefs, values, norms and expectations of the school? By what process did I come to feel like an insider instead of an outsider? Until just recently, I didn't know how, but I knew all of these things had happened. I knew that I somehow managed to gain the respect of my students and engendered the respect, admiration and approval of my colleagues and principals. But it had been twenty years since I first entered Watson Middle school and after having taught English for five years and served as assistant principal for fifteen, these questions still plagued me.

It seemed odd that during the twenty years that I had worked in schools that I had failed to discover the answers to these questions. In all honesty, though, I had developed some tacit answers, but none that I can say were valid. I had observed many teachers come and go during my tenure, many of whom I had reached out to in one way or another. But I really never knew if I was reaching out to them in the most useful ways. My experience tells me that, if twenty years in educational organizations had failed to reveal answers to these plaguing questions, maybe a research project would. I used these questions, then, to frame the research which resulted in this study.

In constructing this study, my purpose was to gather concrete evidence of what it is that new teachers need in order to adjust to an unfamiliar school organization much less painfully. I sought to discover what kinds of help are best and what interventions can orient new teachers to the school and community and provide the instructional and interpersonal support which leads to a smooth transition.

My approach to this study, then, was to identify a school where it had been established that several newcomers were to report and to follow these teachers for the course of the year in order to capture their experience. After having established that twelve new teachers were to report to the school where I worked, I obtained permission to observe and interview them. Six volunteered to participate in the study and six declined. Of the six who volunteered, three were beginning teachers and three were experienced teachers who were either transferred from neighboring schools or returning to the profession after extended absences. This combination provided a basis for comparison. With these variables I could determine what influence prior teaching experience had on the subjects' socialization.

The most difficult facet of this study was to remain cast in my researcher role as the subjects struggled to make sense of the complex organization and learn the ropes. Many times my desire to offer them the help they desperately needed conflicted with my need to avoid contaminating the data. It was important for them to have a typical experience, however, and not be strongly influenced by my presence as participant observer.

I struggled to maintain my researcher role throughout the course of this study, for any teacher who is a newcomer to a school receives my deepest empathy and concern. I have been where they are. Many of us educators have been through that first year in a new school and experienced it virtually alone.

The importance of that first year in a school has been underestimated, not only for beginning teachers, but for veterans as well. I am convinced that the first year in a school organization can make or break a teacher. This first year establishes a pattern of behaviors, feelings, and predispositions that become a part of a teacher's psyche. How successfully or unsuccessfully teachers get through that first year may determine their future orientations and affect their personal and professional growth. Furthermore, I am convinced that a teacher's sense of self in the teacher role can be determined by the quality of that first year experience in a school.

There is much that schools can do to bridge the gap and provide a nurturing environment for new teachers. This research project, from which I developed six case studies, was designed to reveal the true nature of the teachers' first year in the school and allow the reader to explore some ways to provide intervention.

Case studies are valuable pieces of research because of their ability to yield a richness of description and an in-depth treatment of the subject matter that would not be possible using quantitative methods. Case studies allow us to identify with the subjects and gain a clearer understanding of the problems they encounter. Once we understand the nature of these teachers' problems and experiences in the new school, we are much better prepared to seek workable solutions.

Needless to say, I felt that the genre I chose as a vehicle for reporting my research findings should preserve this richness and adequately capture the experience. I first considered presenting my findings as theatre, where the characters re-live those profound experiences and engage the audience emotionally and intellectually. A second consideration involved writing up my findings in the form of a handbook for teachers. I wrote the handbook in its entirety, only to find that it was too prescriptive. Yet, I knew that to present my findings in the traditional dissertation format would serve no purpose except to earn me the degree I sought.

I wanted more. Somehow, I wanted to produce a document that would both capture the true essence of what it means to be a newcomer in an unfamiliar school and tantalize the imagination of student teachers. I wanted the document to edify, inculcate and guide the novice. I wanted to produce a document that would entertain, yet raise the moral consciousness of educators and school practitioners. But most of all, I yearned for broad exposure. A message rarely heard is rarely heeded. Thus, my yearning brought forth an earlier passion that remained unfulfilled. My passion for journalism gave birth to a novel.

This genre allows me to reveal the richness of the data collected and gives readers an avenue through which they can vicariously experience the realities of being a newcomer. A novel has the capacity to capture the experience. Certainly if this novel can help one teacher have a better first year in a school, my purpose will have been fulfilled.

Although this novel is based upon actual occurrences, it is fictional. The names of all characters are pseudonyms and the activities occurring outside of the school are a figment of my imagination. Yet, every event is based upon actual observations and information provided by the participants during the numerous interviews conducted by the researcher. For the most part, information used to create action outside of the school was supplied by the subjects themselves. Typically, once the school day ended so did my research.

There were occasions, however, when research did extend beyond the school day. My major professor charged with overseeing this project, Terry Deal, judiciously scheduled focus group interviews with the subjects at the beginning, middle, and end of this study. These sessions were normally held away from the school site and were designed to validate the data collected and establish some degree of reliability. Professor Deal played an active role in the conduct of these sessions by serving as a devil's advocate as well as assisting in the identification of emerging themes. The high level of trust he established with the subjects also encouraged the sharing of information that the participants may have withheld from the researcher.

The group interview held at the conclusion of this study was a particularly powerful one. Subjects openly shared their impressions of the nature of their socialization and offered some suggestions for change. Thus, all conclusions drawn in this study are corroborated by the subjects themselves. Professor Deal's level of interest and involvement in the study also served as a source of support and inspiration for the group of participants as well as the researcher.

During the course of the year over 40 hours of interviews were conducted, subjects were observed in and out of their classrooms, and the researcher attended their faculty meetings, conferences, PTSA meetings, ball games, and faculty socials. In essence, the researcher became a part of their world and shared in their experience by becoming a participant observer.

The novel as it appears is as close to reality as the researcher could make it without revealing the identities of the subjects. Most of the incidents occurring at the school actually took place. Also, much of the conversation during interview sessions is recorded verbatim from transcriptions.

A concerted effort has been made to make the events realistic because the author wants the reader to be able to walk in the characters' shoes. In support of this effort to strive for realism, several of the subjects very graciously read the first draft and provided helpful feedback. All subjects were given a copy of their complete case study so they could verify the information recorded.

Given the fact that the events are reality-based and data collection strategies employed a form of naturalistic inquiry, this document should be viewed as a naturalistic novel. What is meant by naturalistic is that the research was conducted in the natural habitat of the subjects under study. While engaged in this process of naturalistic inquiry, the researcher actually attempted to gain entry into the subjects' world and be accepted as a native or member of the group.

I am delighted that I was able to cross over into their world, even for short periods of time. To have gained complete acceptance would have been extremely difficult to achieve because of the manner in which my role in the organization was defined. As I look back over their diaries and interview transcriptions, however, I realize that there are times when all of us have forgotten my organizational role and I have become one of them. For these fleeting moments I am grateful, for without them I would not have gained as much valuable information.

In the appendices, you will find several documents that you may find helpful. Appendix A provides a revealing document titled "Students' Expectations of Their Teachers," which resulted from responses to a questionnaire administered to 200 students enrolled in the participants' classes. Two classes from each participating teacher were randomly selected to respond to the questionnaire. As an outgrowth of the questionnaire, a focus-group comprised of twelve of the students who responded to the questionnaire was conducted. From this focus-group, the researcher developed the document entitled "How Students Determine When to Give a Teacher a Hard Time," which appears as Appendix B. For those readers interested in the intricate details of this research, Appendix C provides a list of the specific research questions explored and a description of my methodology. This section is appropriately entitled "The Novel Method." Appendix D provides a review of the related literature. In keeping with the selected genre, I have entitled this section "The Flashback.".

The pages which follow are my best effort to describe what happened to those teachers who were newcomers to the suburban high school where the research was conducted. I hope you will enjoy this novel. The action starts at the school and mounts very quickly so that you become trapped in the world of the lead character, Gail. I do hope that Gail's experience will have a profound effect on you. It certainly did on the researcher. Please keep in mind that Gail does not represent every teacher, but her experience is typical in many ways. Some of what Gail experiences is due to her personal characteristics and the context of her particular teaching situation. Now, I invite you to step into Gail's world.

Chapter 1

A RITE OF PASSAGE

She sees it out of the corner of her eye. As she makes the curve and crosses the bridge, she sees it looming to her right. She slows down. According to the directions she has been given, this should be it. She presses the brake pedal hard and stops in the middle of the street. The large red-brick building captures her full attention. As soon as a horn blows, she looks up and sees the name on the marquee:

Melrose Comprehensive High School
Home of the Roses

Gail Simmons turns into the long driveway, her dark brown eyes getting larger by the moment. She pulls her auburn hair back from her face and tucks it behind her ears so she can see clearly. Although the hot August sun makes her squint, her hands feel as cold as marble against her ear lobes.

As she approaches a deep curve in the driveway, she sees a baseball field and tennis court to her right, a football stadium and swimming pool to her left. There must be three hundred parking spaces. She wonders how many students go to a school this size.

The school is not quite like she imagined. She expected the building to be made of red brick. And it is. She expected the flagpole to be right out front. And it is. But never in a million years would she have been prepared for such splendor.

The red bricks are laid in an interestingly intricate pattern across the front of the building and even form the majestic corridor that she follows to the principal's office. This magnificent building spans at least seven acres and is nestled in a valley surrounded by rolling hillsides resplendent with majestic trees. Never has she seen such a beautiful building as the one which houses Melrose High School.

If she had not followed directions carefully she would have mistaken Melrose for a junior college campus or a corporate headquarters. She can't help but think how wonderful it would be to work in such a beautiful school.

Before she opens the door which leads to the principal's office, she removes a handkerchief from her purse and wipes her brow. Her bluntly-cut bangs fall right back in place. Feeling confident and determined that she will land her first teaching job, she opens the door.

The door closes very quietly, but a cheerful secretary peers over the trophies lined across the counter as if she is expecting someone.

"Good morning. Gail Simmons?"

"Yes." Gail takes a deep breath and swallows hard, trying desperately to keep her heart from racing. She eases her trembling hand from the counter and rubs it against her black skirt, thankful that the trophies hide her nervousness. She wants so much to make a good impression.

"Dr. Reed is expecting you. May I get you some coffee?"

"No, thank you."

"Let me tell him you are here."

Gail wants to delay her, but she moves too quickly. Her mouth and throat suddenly feel dry. She licks her lips and the cherry wine flavor of her lipstick tastes bitter. Now she needs something to get the bitter taste out of her mouth.

Gail swallows and takes a deep breath. The receptionist comes back, saying, "Dr. Reed will see you now, Miss Simmons. Just follow me." Gail's feet and legs feel numb, lifeless. A few seconds later her feet are walking on plush, royal blue carpet.

Dr. Reed stands and extends his hand as Gail enters. He has a twinkle in his right eye which Gail finds hard to read, but otherwise, Dr. Reed fits her perception of the typical principal. Dr. Reed is tall and slender, with a slightly bulging stomach. A few strands of gray appear around his temples, and a bald spot in the middle of his scalp can no longer be hidden by his thin, dark hair. His sharp, jutting jawline gives his rather boyish face an air of authority that Gail finds intimidating.

"Have a seat." He motions for her to sit in the chair directly in front of his desk. "Is it Miss or Mrs. Simmons?"

Happy that he started with a simple question, Gail answers readily. "It's Miss. I'm divorced, so I've changed back to my maiden name, but . . ."

Without giving her time to finish, he wheels around and dials the phone behind his desk. Gail wonders if she has said the wrong thing. "Is Mrs. Rossman on the way?" he asks. "Ok. I'll wait a few minutes, then. Thank you." As quickly as he puts the phone back on the hook, he swings his chair back around facing Gail.

"Do you have any children?" he asks.

"No," she answers nervously. "I've always wanted children, though." Gail picks a piece of lint from her black skirt, wondering how it had escaped her scrutiny.

"Well," Dr. Reed says with a boyish grin, "being divorced doesn't help much, does it?"

Gail pauses, not knowing how to read the twinkle in his eye or the grin. Just as she is about to open her mouth to respond, a petite, brown-skinned woman appears in the doorway.

"Hello, my name is Cheryl Rossman." She extends her hand, smiles very warmly, and sits to the right of Dr. Reed's desk. There is a genuineness in her smile that Gail finds refreshing. Her royal blue suit extends almost down to her ankles and matches her royal blue pumps.

"Mrs. Rossman is the curriculum principal here at Melrose," Dr. Reed explains. "The two of us have always worked together on hiring new teachers and organizing the school." Gail is surprised that Cheryl Rossman is an assistant principal. She seems much too young. Gail is not sure what curriculum principals do, but she is certainly interested in seeing how any administrator of the female gender functions. She remembers that all the principals at the high school she attended were male.

Gail hands Dr. Reed and Cheryl Rossman her resume and waits in silence while they read it. Suddenly Dr. Reed breaks the silence. "I see you taught at Ambrosia some time ago."

Gail, remembering her sister's advice to sell herself, sits up very straight and attempts to look in his eyes, but he continues looking at her resume. She catches Mrs. Rossman's gaze for just a moment and looks back at Dr. Reed. He appears to be reading yet another document from his desk.

"Yes. I really enjoyed that. It was a substitute teaching position for someone who was on maternity leave. I believe her name was Wilma Berry. Her students were so appreciative of everything I did for them. That was a great experience."

"Yes. Wilma Berry is working for us now," Cheryl Rossman states. "What other experience have you had in working with young people?" she asks.

"Well, none really. I've worked with college students at Tuskegee."

"So, why do you want to teach?" Cheryl turns toward Gail.

Gail feels confident in her decision and responds eagerly. "After serving as a substitute, I went into sales for a publishing company. I enjoyed it, and I didn't exactly get burned out on it. It just didn't seem very important to me anymore. Sales just kept going on day after day. The business world kept going on and on and I didn't feel I was making a real big difference to anyone."

Cheryl interrupts, "Why not?"

"I like to help people, and I like being in contact with people. I was in contact with people, but it was so scattered. It was like you're here and there and just all over the place. Some customers you get to know and you may help some, but it's not like teaching. This is why I really just want to get back into teaching. After substitute teaching at Ambrosia High there wasn't a position available, so I just went on and did something else. I enjoyed sales and the money was good."

Dr. Reed interrupts. "The money was better than what you'll be getting here, I would think!"

"It's hard to say in a way because I had an expense account. With that, it may have been close to $10,000.00 more. But I won't be spending that much. I'm not going to be staying in hotels, so it's hard to calculate. As far as the salary goes, there is about a four or five thousand dollar difference. Money is important to me, but it's not critical."

"So what's more important to you?" Cheryl Rossman asks.

Gail answers without hesitation. "When I'm interested in something. When I'm involved with people instead of just things. And that's the way it was with sales. It was just a product, not people."

Gail can tell that she has struck a positive chord with Cheryl Rossman, who nods her head in agreement. It is not as easy to read Dr. Reed's response. He keeps his head down most of the time, seeming somewhat disinterested in the conversation since the subject has shifted from money to something less substantive.

Cheryl probes Gail further about her decision to teach. "It's certainly commendable that you're willing to come back to teaching after having been out of the classroom for ten years. Are you prepared to deal with the changes which have occurred?"

Gail clears her throat and tucks a lock of her dark, shoulder-length hair behind her left ear. "Well, I haven't been totally isolated from public school for ten years. Both my parents were teachers. In fact, my father was a principal here in Camden County and my mother taught elementary school for thirty-two years. I've grown up in a teaching family and helped grade papers and so forth. So I've heard all the stories about what happens in schools."

Cheryl appears to be listening intently. Gail is not sure she has been convincing enough, so she continues. "In fact, I have a sister who was recently elected 'Teacher of the Year' at one of the magnet schools. She really does a great job, so I feel that I can do it, too. I'd like to at least give it a try. Teaching is a family tradition."

"I see," Cheryl says, pausing long enough for Dr. Reed to comment.

"Miss Simmons," Dr. Reed announces rather hurriedly. "Melrose is a comprehensive high school which means it is much larger than Ambrosia. We have 1,700 students in this building which spans seven and one-half acres, and we teach academic and vocational subjects. We're predominantly black, but our black population represents the middle class while our white population resides in a rural, less affluent community. So we're different from most of the system's other schools in that respect. Right now we are seventy-five percent black and twenty-five percent white. We are departmentalized and we have four different grade schools. You will be assigned to one of these grade schools and that principal will evaluate you. Now, Mrs. Rossman will tell you what you will be teaching."

Gail feels an enormous sense of relief and pride. She smiles broadly as Cheryl flips several pages of the faculty schedule she has held on her lap during the interview. Gail's first inclination is to stand up and shake Dr. Reed's hand, but she struggles to maintain composure. She watches Cheryl closely as she stops turning pages and pauses.

"Let's see," Cheryl says, appearing a bit perplexed. "At this point, we only have four firm classes for you. We should be able to determine what your fifth class will be in just a few days. Right now I'm looking at one ninth grade standard English class, two eleventh grade Proficiency English classes, and one career education class."

"We have an advanced placement class we need to split, don't we?" Dr. Reed asks.

"Yes, but. . . ."

Dr. Reed interrupts, "Miss Simmons, you have come to us highly recommended and your credentials are exceptionally strong. Would you like to teach an advanced placement class?" he asks.

By now, the pounding in Gail's ears almost drowns the sound of Dr. Reed's voice. She has never felt such excitement.

"Oh, yes! Yes, sir! I would love to teach an advanced placement class. I'll need to see a copy of the textbook, though."

Gail is surprised because she knows that to assign a new teacher to an advanced placement class violates the established pecking order. Her sister has already prepared her for the worst by telling her not to expect good classes her first year. She has told her that she must earn the right to teach upper level classes and the best students by putting in her time and paying her dues. According to her sister, proving yourself capable of teaching the worst classes and unmotivated students is a rite of passage that all teachers must endure.

"Mrs. Rossman will take you to your room now and introduce you to the department chair who will give you a copy of the textbooks you will need." Gail is smiling unabashedly, now.

Cheryl extends her hand to Gail as they turn to leave Dr. Reed's office, "Welcome to Melrose!" Cheryl states, quite sincerely. "You're going to love it here. Let's go meet Mrs. Easley first; then I will take you to your room."

Gail is intimidated by the sheer size of the building once they leave the main office suite. As they enter the main lobby just outside the office, she tries to compare the size of Melrose with the high school she had attended. She feels that her entire school would fit into the lobby of this building.

She and Cheryl take an elevator to the second floor. As they get off the elevator and proceed down the corridor Cheryl explains how each area of the building is color coded. The English, Foreign Language, and Social Studies wing is surrounded by a light brown carpet. Other areas of the building are covered with red, green, or orange carpet. The entire building is colorful. Student lockers are a bright, lemon yellow and the assistant principals' offices are surrounded by glass so that they can have a clear view of the locker areas at all times. Melrose is certainly a beautiful place to work. Gail can hardly wait to see her classroom.

As Cheryl opens the door to Mrs. Easley's room, Gail cannot help but notice how spacious it is. Rows of very colorful, modern, metal desks line the carpeted floor. Mrs. Easley's desk and several file cabinets match the students' desks. The left wall is lined with bookshelves containing textbooks, classics, and paperbacks of every kind. The right wall is lined with colorful file cabinets and an attractively decorated bulletin board. What would have normally been the back wall of the classroom is an entire wall of windows. Through the windows Gail can see into the courtyard and cafeteria which are also surrounded by stationary glass windows. Three medium-sized blackboards are situated directly behind Mrs. Easley's desk. Gail's mind goes back to her years as a student in a very different classroom setting several years earlier. Just as she is about to comment about the differences she notices, a rather plump, rosy-cheeked Mrs. Easley enters the room.

"Good morning, Mrs. Rossman. How are you? I was just down at the main office and Dr. Reed told me you were on your way up to see me." Mrs. Easley is visibly out of breath; yet she enunciates every word perfectly. "I understand we have a new member of our department. Welcome to the 'Rose'."

"This is Miss Gail Simmons. She'll be teaching the unassigned courses in the department and will probably be relieving you of part of that large A.P. class."

"Thank you, thank you!" Mrs. Easley exclaims enthusiastically. "I was wondering how I was going to manage thirty-nine A.P. students all in the same class period. Let me suggest that we plan to split that group first thing tomorrow morning. Once bonding occurs, they really hate to leave their classmates. It will be so much easier on you, too, if they know you are their teacher from the very beginning." The smell of sweet honeysuckle permeates the air as Mrs. Easley moves about the room.

Gail is not quite certain she will be prepared to teach an A.P. class overnight, but she does not want to appear incompetent. She appreciates the fact that everyone is demonstrating such confidence in her abilities. She certainly does not want to do anything to destroy their confidence.

Cheryl diplomatically dismisses herself and leaves Gail in the hands of Mrs. Easley. Gail finds the time with Mrs. Easley well-spent. By the time Cheryl reappears to show Gail to her room, she is loaded down with books, teachers' editions, and resource manuals. She realizes it will be impossible to remember half of what Mrs. Easley has told her and wishes she had brought along a tape recorder.

"Well, Miss Simmons, I should have brought you a cart shouldn't I?" Cheryl says jokingly.

"Mrs. Easley certainly gave me a lot of information. She is just wonderful. How long has she been here?" Gail asks.

"Mrs. Easley helped to open this school ten years ago. She has a wealth of information and knowledge to share. All you have to do is avail yourself. She is the most highly regarded teacher in the building and Dr. Reed counts on her to write the reports that go out from the school. She is an excellent writer and an expert in the area of literary criticism. Aside from serving as chair for the largest department in the school, she also chairs several system-wide committees and conducts summer workshops."

"Umm . . . I should spend a lot of time with her, then." Gail says.

"Absolutely. Absolutely. Did she tell you that there are three other new members of the department?"

"Oh, yes. She did. I can't wait to meet them."

A moment later, Gail forgets her excitement about meeting the other newcomers. "Here we are." Cheryl says, finally showing her the classroom wherein she is expected to practice her craft. Gail catches her breath. There is a stark difference in Gail's room and Mrs. Easley's. There are no colorful student desks or neatly arranged rows of blackboard space. There are no stationary windows. In fact, there are no windows at all. The uncarpeted room is long and narrow instead of wide and spacious. Gail recognizes the stale, closet-like odor that signals the room has not been used for a while.

The desk at the front of the room which is designated for Gail is only half as large as Mrs. Easley's and looks very similar to the one her high school English teacher used. A battered stool in one corner of the room looks like an Oreo cookie from which some hungry mice have taken several bites and abandoned in fear and desperation. The one file cabinet is a bright orange, while the student desks are the vanilla colored variety reminiscent of the desks Gail occupied when she attended high school. Gail's room contains only one scant blackboard and a small bulletin board. The chatter of adult voices which can easily be heard through the walls gives Gail a start.

"Don't mind that," Cheryl explains. "This room is located between two workrooms. The language arts workroom is to the left and the social studies workroom is located to the right. You'll find that once school is in session, there will be little opportunity for large groups of teachers to occupy the workrooms and make small talk. One advantage for you is that you can store some of your materials in the workrooms and have easy access to copy machines and just about anything else you might need at the spur of the moment. We thought this room would be workable for you because your classes are relatively small and the groups you have will really not require a lot of space." Gail stands motionless and speechless as Cheryl continues.

"Take a few moments to get settled in. If you need anything, feel free to ask Mrs. Easley or come to the office. At 10:00 o'clock this morning I will be meeting with you and all of our new teachers for orientation. That meeting will be held in the conference room down in the main office. Are there any questions?" Gail shakes her head to indicate that there are none. "Well, I shall see you at ten o'clock sharp."

As Cheryl makes her retreat, Gail looks at the clock on the wall. It is already half past nine.

Thought Questions

Chapter 1 – Rites of Passage

1. What themes are emerging in this first chapter?

2. How would you feel if you were Gail?

3. What suggestions do you have for Gail, at this point?

4. Why do you think this chapter is titled "Rites of Passage?"

5. What rites of passage are relevant to Gail's experience?

Chapter 2

THORNS

The main office conference room is quiet. A long, rectangular conference table surrounded by ten blue upholstered chairs occupies most of the space. Although small, the room is attractively decorated. The ten blue upholstered chairs match the blue carpet. The first thing Gail sees upon entering the conference room is the blue and gold flag, prominently displayed on the back wall, which carries the inscription "Mayor's Excellence Award".

There are a couple of portraits representing some outstanding landmarks of the community of which Melrose is a part. One is a picture of the state capitol building, another a portrait of the Andrew Jackson Building. On the wall facing the head of the conference table is a breathtaking picture of a huge, red rose. Its brilliance overtakes the room. The gold plated sign mounted against the frame reads "Our Mascot". Another wall contains a large map detailing the geographical boundaries of the school zone.

A bouquet of silk, red roses which Gail assumes serves as the centerpiece for the conference table has been placed on an adjacent coffee table in the corner. A large tray of assorted cookies, a small bowl of lime-colored punch, and red napkins now occupy center stage and await the arrival of the new teachers who are about to receive their official orientation to Melrose Comprehensive High School. Not knowing where she is expected to sit around the huge table, Gail retreats to the main office reception area to wait for others to assemble.

The main office quiet is disrupted by the arrival of Patsy Miller at 9:46. Patsy is a vivacious, very attractive blond. Her high-pitched voice cuts through the quiet as she enters.

"Hi! You must be new. I'm Patsy Miller and I can answer any questions you have about this school. I have taught here for an entire school year. Believe me, you will love it!"

"Was it your first year to teach?" Gail asks.

"Yep. But let me tell ya, it was a breeze. I had absolutely no problems. Teaching is the cushiest job I have ever had. Everyone just leaves you alone to do whatever you want to do. I guess I'm luckier than most, though, because Mrs. Easley has really looked out for me."

"In what respect?" Gail asks with interest.

"See, I started out doing my student teaching under Mrs. Easley. Well, she became ill before the end of the semester and I had to close out for her. I did everything exactly as she told me and even graded all of the exams. When Dr. Reed learned that she wouldn't be back until the fall, he asked me if I'd like to stay as her substitute for the rest of the year."

"I see," Gail says.

Patsy's green eyes are bright and her voice animated as she continues. "I was sure Mrs. Easley put in a good word for me when Dr. Reed called to tell me that he had an opening. I have known I had this job all summer long."

"That's great. I just found out this morning." Gail says.

"You see," Patsy states with confidence. "It's all in who you know."

Patsy demonstrates a great deal of self-assurance and confidence as she approaches assistant principal, Cheryl Rossman, who enters the office to begin the orientation session for the teachers who are new to Melrose.

"Cheryl," she begins, with little concern for formalities, "Do I need to attend the meeting? Since I've been here for a while, I'm not really new, you know."

"I realize you spent ten weeks here last fall, but that was student teaching. You also took over Mrs. Easlely's position for the spring, and we really do appreciate all of your hard work. Your responsibilities will be a bit different now that you are one of us. We were really pleased with your performance last year and we appreciate everything you did for the school during Mrs. Easley's absence, but I would really like for you to sit in on this meeting if for no other reason than to assist me in answering some of the others' questions. I also need to tell you about a special project I would like you to participate in this year. Ok?"

"You have to watch that Ms. Rossman." Patsy tells Gail. "The lady has the ability to be straightforward, authoritative, and nurturing all at the same time. Her smile will win you over every time, tearing down all your defenses."

Patsy occupies a seat in the outer office area right next to Gail, but she seems to find it difficult to sit for long. The endless rows of athletic trophies lined across the counter capture her attention. She notices other trophies and plaques mounted against the wall surrounding the receptionist's work station. The immense collection is quite impressive. Patsy gets up to take a closer look.

"Boy!" She shrieks in a girlish tone. "Wonder how many of these trophies Danny won for this school?"

Mrs. Jones, the receptionist, knows exactly who she is talking about. "Danny Slaughter left four trophies. One for every year he played. We sure will miss him. He was a good one! But I'm sure Coach Moss will find another one to take his place. You can bet your bottom dollar that he's outside looking the freshman team over right now. Ever since Coach Moss took over the football team, we've gone to the state, and he's not gonna' rest easy until he knows we've got the potential to go again this year. Yeah, he's a great coach!"

"How long has he been here?" Patsy asks with interest.

"He's been here about seven years, and we've been to the state for six", says Dr. Reed who could easily hear the conversation from his office. "You know it takes a coach at least a year to build a winning team. Coach Moss came right after Coach Dover retired. And we will probably go to the state again this year because old Sammy Wade is a pretty good player. Sammy's a senior this year, so he should be ready to take over as quarterback. We're probably going to the state in basketball this year, too. We've got several top scorers on that basketball team."

"Wow! That would be wonderful! It looks like we may also be doing well in track and field," Patsy says. Dr. Reed has disappeared back into the seclusion of his office as quickly as he emerged, but Mrs. Jones can certainly speak on the topic at hand.

"Now, you know, we have never taken a back seat when it comes to track and field. Our girls' track team has won the state championship ever since this school opened ten years ago."

"You have got to be kidding!" Patsy exclaims in amazement. "The students here are really great, aren't they?"

"Yep! They're tops. We've had some good ones come and go. I've been here since the first day the school opened and I can still remember a lot of them. We've not only had some good kids in football, basketball, and track; we've had some good ones in cross country, golf, baseball, and wrestling, too. And Dr. Reed just loves it when we win. You'll see, once you stay around here long enough. We've got the best athletes in town!"

The evidence is convincing. Gail listens with great interest and feels that she is really lucky to be teaching at a school where there is such pride and motivation to succeed. She only wishes that she knew as much as Patsy does or could be just as confident.

It is now very close to 10:00 and Gail fears that most of the other newcomers have assembled in the conference room. Patsy is so engrossed in viewing the vast array of trophies and plaques on display that Gail has to remind her of the time.

Cheryl is already in the conference room chatting with the new teachers when they enter. Patsy and Gail occupy the two remaining seats where the neatly arranged stacks of orientation materials are still undisturbed. Gail is relieved that she has come in before the meeting starts.

Cheryl does not hesitate to start the meeting at exactly 10:00. Deliberately attempting to model the behavior she expects, Cheryl begins by introducing herself and describing her role as curriculum principal. She explains that she taught English for five years and was promoted to an assistant principal at the same school where she was teaching. She describes how she worked as a coordinator of discipline for two years and then moved into the position at Melrose. At the conclusion of Cheryl's remarks, it is obvious that her primary interest lies in the improvement of instruction and in supporting the instructional program.

"As long as you do what we expect in the classroom, you have my total support," she concludes. "Now, I would like for each of you to introduce yourselves. We'll let you begin, Gail. This is Gail Simmons, everyone. Gail just arrived this morning and is the newest member of our faculty. Gail brings our total number of newcomers up to ten. She has been a sales representative for a major book publisher for years, and she has become somewhat disenchanted with the competitive nature of the industry and decided to give teaching a try. Is that correct, Gail?"

Gail's voice is barely audible as she responds. "Yes, I guess you could say that. The thing that concerned me most was that I didn't feel I was helping anyone by selling books. I really do want to help people, you know. I consider teaching an important and vital profession, and I can think of no better way to help people than through teaching."

"Ok. So, what other experiences have you had that you would like to share with the group?" Cheryl asks.

"Well . . . I worked as a librarian at a community college and at a university before I decided to go into sales." Her soft voice comes to a stop just as a soft knock is heard at the door.

Mrs. Rossman, you have a phone call," Mrs. Jones announces. "I thought you would like to take it, since it's long distance."

"Yes, I would." Cheryl looks a bit frustrated as she glances at her watch. "You all continue to introduce yourselves. I will be back shortly. Patsy, why don't you go next?"

"Hi! My name is Patricia Miller, but please call me Patsy. I am a little bit ahead of the rest of you guys because I have spent almost an entire year here already. I completed my student teaching here on last year under Mrs. Easley. You have missed a real treat if you haven't met her yet. She is just wonderful. But, anyway, because she gave me such a fantastic evaluation, Cheryl and Dr. Reed had enough confidence in me to give me the first teaching position that became available in the department. And I have the most wonderful schedule! I could not believe it when Dr. Reed told me that I would be teaching senior English and coaching forensics. I have to be the luckiest teacher in the world. And, let me tell you, you are just going to love working here. This is the best school. Cheryl Rossman will knock herself out trying to help you. But you'd better be doing what you're supposed to do. And Dr. Reed will also support you and give you a pat on the back every now and then. You just have to know when he's having a bad day and leave him alone on those days. . . ."

Patsy is interrupted by a bright-eyed teacher sitting directly across from her. "Well, my name is Roxanne Baker, and I just want to say to you, Patsy, that I am glad you have been assigned the forensics instead of me. Dr. Reed had asked me about it, but I didn't want to take it unless I just had to. I just can't imagine coming to a school this size and coaching the forensics team your first year." Gail is amazed at how fast Roxanne talks.

"Well, it depends upon how badly you want this job," says Patsy. "I decided I was going to do whatever I had to do just to get my foot in the door. Once you've been here for a while, then you can afford to be selective. I wasn't stupid enough to refuse. Now you look quite a bit older than I am. Maybe you don't have to worry about keeping your job."

Gail senses that Patsy's comments have angered Roxanne. Roxanne leans toward Patsy as she continues, her eyes glaring.

"I'm very happy to be at Melrose also," Roxanne continues, "because I have been trying to get the opportunity to teach in a high school for several years. I have requested one transfer after another and a position finally opened up. I'm sure personnel just got tired of looking at my request each year and finally decided to let me have what I wanted. The only regret I have is that I don't have a room. But if I had to choose between teaching forensics and having a room of my own, I'd rather go without a room this year. It's just that I resent the fact that Dr. Reed or someone told the personnel director that I wasn't qualified to teach forensics just so you could get a job. I've been teaching at the middle school for four years and have coached forensics before, so I know I'm better qualified than someone who has never taught before."

Several members of the group raise their hands to respond, but no one can stop Roxanne. "The only reason I wanted to come to this school, or any high school for that matter, was to be able to teach literature. At the middle school level, we spend eighty percent of our time teaching grammar. It's not that I don't care for grammar, it's just that I studied all of this literature for my master's degree and I haven't been able to use all that knowledge. I would like to use it before I forget it, you know."

"We're supposed to teach quite a lot of grammar here too, Roxanne", Patsy interjects. "But, of course, there's no way Cheryl Rossman or any of the other administrators can keep up with everything that's going on in your classroom."

"Oh, pardon me. All this discussion about forensics and having no room is so interesting I forgot it was my turn," says another woman who introduces herself as Lucy Cummings. "I do have a room, fortunately. I don't know how I could manage without one, really. But I am very happy to be here because I am much closer to home now. My husband and I have just moved into our new home right down the street from here and we just love this community. We have two daughters, so this arrangement is working out perfectly for us. Since I won't have to drive so far, I can pick the girls up from school and still have time to come back and see my students participate in ball games and other extracurricular activities. It's amazing how important it is for students to see us at their activities, so I plan to come back quite often. It will help me get more out of them in the classroom. I have been in this school system for eleven years, but I've just come off maternity leave. I took an extended maternity leave for three years. I just feel very lucky to be here because, first of all, personnel called me and told me I would have to work in a middle school because there were no openings at the high school level. So I told them I would resign before I went to a middle school to teach eighth graders. You know how they think you're dumb? If I were a new teacher I would do it just to get my foot in the door, but I've been teaching a while and I know better. I've already been through that nightmare and I'm not going to repeat it. Sure enough, a couple of days later they called me back and suddenly there were all these openings at the high school level. They could even give me my choice of schools. Well, anyway, I chose Melrose because it was closer, although I don't know much about it. But, when I came in for my interview with Dr. Reed he told me I would have to do the school newspaper and yearbook. I told him I couldn't do it, but I understood if he couldn't take me for that reason. So I felt real lucky when I got this job. I feel real fortunate just to be here."

Gail looks at Lucy Cummings and wonders how she can possibly have the energy to care for two daughters. She is so tiny that Gail is suspicious that she is anorexic. Gail wonders when Dr. Reed is going to approach her about an extra assignment. "It could be that the A.P. class is it," she thinks.

Suddenly a heavy, masculine voice penetrates the atmosphere. "Since I am the only male in this group and also the only one who will not be teaching English, I felt it was appropriate for me to be the last to introduce myself." The group, feeling very relaxed now, laughs heartily just as Cheryl returns. Cheryl smiles and looks pleased that she has succeeded in establishing the perfect climate for the rest of her orientation session.

The male voice continues. "My name is Clyde Reynolds. I don't seem to have very much in common with the rest of you except the fact that I have taught before. It was a long time ago, however, eight years ago as a matter of fact. I teach science and have been given five classes of freshman science this year. I quit teaching eight years ago in order to make more money to support my wife and new baby. I started working in industry because the money was so much better. I have worked at the Coca-Cola Company and at AVCO in management. I left AVCO after being laid off and decided I would come back to what I really enjoy doing—teaching."

There is a long pause, so Gail assumes Clyde is finished. The group appears to be waiting for more, but something in Clyde's demeanor lets Gail know that he is not willing to share anymore. The far-away look in his eyes lets Gail know that his mind is not really on the subject at hand. Gail wonders if he has returned to teaching as a last resort. She feels sorry for people who are forced to leave their jobs. Cheryl clears her throat and goes on to the next item on the agenda.

For the next forty-five minutes Cheryl covers a lot of territory. She explains Melrose's organizational structure and describes the community. She gives each teacher a handbook which details all the operational procedures and instructional expectations. Because of the time limitations, she covers only the most important areas in the teacher handbook and asks that they read all other sections at their leisure. She takes great pains to explain how they are to execute the various forms that must be submitted at specified times and under certain circumstances. She tries to leave no stone unturned, yet Gail realizes that it is virtually impossible to remember everything that Cheryl has told them. She only hopes that someone will be available to answer her questions when uncertainties arise.

Right before closing, Cheryl digresses momentarily to discuss a special project with the group. "For some time now, I have been concerned about what happens to new teachers when they are assigned to large, comprehensive high schools such as this one. Although most of you are veterans who have several years of teaching experience, this first year at Melrose is not going to be easy for any of you. I would like to provide as much help as I can, but I also need your help so that we can determine exactly what it is that new teachers need when they are placed in an unfamiliar school environment."

Cheryl watches their faces closely and continues, "I invite you to participate in a research project with me that will encompass the entire school year. It will require at least an hour of your time every other week during a six weeks period, although more time may be required occasionally. Initially, I will need to meet with you for one hour every week or so to assess the situation. I would like to follow you closely during this first year to determine how you learn the ropes and adjust to the new setting. I will need to do some shadowing, visit your classroom and interview you several times. The interview will need to be audiotaped unless you object, and the project will be supervised by Hillman University. The advantage for you exists in the fact that you will have access to an insider who knows quite a bit about the organization and may be able to answer your questions as they arise. Although I want you to have a typical experience, I will provide as much help as I can without contaminating the data. Now, I do not want you to feel obligated to participate because you are going to be very busy. What I am going to do is leave with you this questionnaire. If you wish to participate, simply complete the questionnaire and return it. If you fail to return it within the next day or so, I will understand that you do not wish to participate and I will not communicate with you regarding this matter any further."

"Sounds like an interesting project!" Patsy exclaims. "You can count me in!"

Cheryl looks at her watch. It is 11:30 and time for the session to end. She extends a final welcome to the group and turns them over to the faculty advisor for a tour of the building. As they leave the conference room, Roxanne turns to Patsy and asks, "Are you also doing the school newspaper and yearbook?"

"Nope." She tosses her blond hair. "Dr. Reed probably gave those to Gail Simmons. She's the newest kid on the block!"

Thought Questions

Chapter 2 – Thorns

1. What thorny issues arise in Chapter 2?

2. Imagine you are Gail Simmons. How would you respond if you were asked to serve as sponsor of the yearbook and/or school newspaper? Provide justification for your response.

3. What is your impression of the two administrators, Cheryl Rossman and Dr. Reed? How would you describe their leadership styles?

Chapter 3

AN AWAKENING

Gail checks the clock beside her bed for the twentieth time to make sure she has not overslept. Wondering if the time reflected on the tiny clock is correct, she gets up and gingerly moves the pink curtain to one side in order to peer out the window. The darkness conceals everything. It is hard to believe, but she knows that by the time her alarm sounds at five o'clock the darkness will have been overtaken by daylight. Gail gets back into bed anticipating more sleeplessness. For thirty more minutes she tugs at the pillows, tosses, and conjures up images of what her first day with the students at Melrose Comprehensive High School will be like. As the dull buzzing of the alarm clock pierces through the quiet of day, Gail rises and wraps herself in her warm robe.

She has not known such nervousness since she first entered elementary school. Gail resorts to what she has always done to calm her nerves. She kneels at her bedside and whispers a short prayer, then practices her yoga. It is 5:15 before Gail faces herself in the bathroom mirror and she is not pleased with what she sees. Her eyes are red and eyelids puffy; her face looks hollow; and her skin is pale. When she splashes cold water on her eyes they sting and burn until tears come.

After a long shower and a breakfast of cold cereal and milk, Gail looks and feels better. She has dressed carefully, hoping to make a good impression on her students. "If only the first period class were not the A.P. students," she thinks. "That group really frightens me, but I must not let anyone know. This is a chance of a lifetime and I must not blow it. The A.P. students are the smartest kids in the school, but they're also the best behaved. Besides, Mrs. Easley will tell me everything to do today. Right? Right. Tomorrow I will have a better handle on things. Tomorrow I will be prepared. Oh, wait, why am I worried? The first day of school is always a half day for students," she remembers. "Oh great! That means I will have the rest of the day to plan for tomorrow. Everything is going to work out fine, just fine!"

Having convinced herself that everything will be fine, Gail picks up her class roll book, course descriptions and the teacher handbook and shoves them into her leather briefcase. The twenty minute drive to Melrose is relaxing and therapeutic. Gail enjoys the beautiful suburban area surrounded by rolling hills and gently sloping valleys. Newly constructed homes with well-manicured lawns are only a few blocks from the school. Gail is captivated by the beautiful trees surrounding the back of the school.

Gail pulls into the faculty parking lot at 6:30 a.m., thinking she is relatively early. But most faculty members have arrived already. Several colorful, well-lettered signs posted on the front doors provide instructions for students and their parents: **ALL NEW STUDENTS REPORT TO THE GYMNASIUM.** An arrow points out the direction of the gymnasium. **ALL FORMER STUDENTS REPORT TO THE CAFETERIA. REPORT TO THE LIBRARY FOR REGISTRATION.** An arrow points out the direction of the library and gymnasium. As Gail walks into the main lobby, she sees small pockets of students talking. Several students are accompanied by a parent. The anticipation in their eyes leads her to believe that they either have not read the signs posted on the front doors or have chosen to ignore them. At any rate, Gail feels she doesn't have time to worry about anyone else. She has to concentrate on her own survival.

Following the dictates that Cheryl Rossman outlined in orientation on the previous day, Gail signs her name on the roster designated for members of the Twelfth Grade School. Other teachers file in and sign rosters as well. The rosters are all color-coded. The Twelfth Grade School roster is blue, the Eleventh Grade School roster is pink, the Tenth Grade School roster is yellow, and the Ninth Grade School roster is green. Gail looks at the roster closely as she signs her name, making sure she jots down the name of the principal, Peter Clinard, which is listed at the top of the roster. She remembers that Dr. Reed has told her that the principal will evaluate her. She certainly wants to stay on good terms with this gentleman. Having signed her name, she looks around for some sign indicating what she should do next, but there is none. Is she expected to go to her room? Is there a special meeting place for teachers, or should she wait in the main office for instructions?

The teachers who come in hurriedly sign their names, speak to the receptionist, check the long rows of mailboxes and make a quick exit. She moves closer to the rows of mailboxes and notices they are in alphabetical order. She looks for Simmons, but there is no mailbox labeled with her name. Neither is her name typed on the School Roster she signed. While she has to sign her full name, the old-timers only have to place their initials by their names. After all, she is a newcomer. She is certain it will take a day or two for these small details to be taken care of.

"Let's see, Miss Simmons," Mrs. Jones, the receptionist says. "You are assigned to room 239. Let me get Joey Miller to show you to your room. Just one moment." Through the glass windows which surround the office, Mrs. Jones motions for Joey and he moves immediately into the office area. Joey's brown eyes sparkle as he sees Mrs. Jones.

"Hi, Mrs. Jones! Do you want me?" His voice is polite, yet somewhat apprehensive.

"Yes, Joey, I want you to meet one of our new teachers, Miss Simmons. She will be teaching English this year and has been assigned to room 239. You know where that is, don't you? Will you please escort her to that area for me?"

"Yes ma'am," Joey says with a lopsided smile, "I will take care of her. No problem." He immediately grabs Gail's briefcase and opens the door for her to exit the main office. The lobby is now filled with large numbers of students who are chatting, exchanging high fives and hugs.

The collage of faces that Gail sees is mostly black. Joey has on Calvin Klein jeans, a silk shirt and a pair of designer shoes. A white, male student who calls out Joey's name as he passes has on a T-shirt, faded out jeans, and sandals. A black male student has on a pair of unlaced high-top sneakers. Several students who decided to dress up for the occasion wear high heels, frilly dresses or expensive suits and ties. The smell of expensive perfumes and colognes permeate the atmosphere, interrupted by occasional bursts of hair spray.

As Gail and Joey go up the steps leading to the second floor, Dr. Reed's voice can be heard on the intercom reminding students and parents of the instructions which are spelled out on the various signs posted throughout the building. The halls beyond the lobby remain quiet, except for the voices of teachers who scurry around making last minute preparations for the arrival of their students.

"I didn't know anyone taught in room 239," Joey says. "Are you sure you are assigned to 239?"

"Yes, I am," Gail answers. "Here we are. Oh, no. It looks like the door is locked, and I am afraid I don't have a key!"

"Don't worry about a thing, Miss Simmons. I know exactly where to go to get you a key. Just stay right here until I get back!" As Joey disappears around the corner, Gail breathes a sigh of relief. At least Mrs. Jones knew what she was doing when she called for Joey. Within five minutes, Joey returns with the head custodian, Mr. Fanroy.

"You need to tell them to git' you a key to this room," Mr Fanroy states, matter-of-factly. "We may not be around to open up for you every morning."

"Who do I see about a key?" Gail inquires.

"Dr. Reed has a key to every room in this building, just like I do. I made one key for myself and one key for him, just like he told me. And in order for me to make a duplikit' key I have to git' his permission. So you need to talk to him today and let me know. You goin' be here for a while or is you a substitute?"

"I plan to be here for a while," Gail says. "I was hired just yesterday."

"Well, I'm sho' we goin' have to make a duplikit key, 'cause nobody's taught in this room befo'. This used to be a bookroom. They got so many students here, they done run out of rooms. I figured Mrs. Rossman was goin' put somebody in this room when she had us to set it up las' week."

"Well, thank you, sir" Gail says.

"You welcome," Mr. Fanroy says. "Just check on that key soon as you kin. Hear?"

"I certainly will, sir," Gail promises. The sound of two short beeps permeates the environment, making Gail's skin crawl. Mr. Fanroy disappears into oblivion.

"Those beeps are a page for Mr. Fanroy, that's all," Joey explains. He's always real busy the first week or so after school starts. He's constantly on call. He's pretty edgy sometimes, but he's a good person to get to know. He looks out for several of the teachers around here. If you are nice to him, he'll be nice to you. If you ask him right he might be able to get you some new desks and chairs. These look kinda' beat up to me." A loud buzzer sounds for about ten seconds.

"Well, there goes the bell. I'll have to go now. You have a good day, Miss Simmons." Joey darts out the door, obviously in a rush, but sticks his head back in momentarily. "Oh, by the way, welcome to the Rose!" Gail wonders what Joey means by being nice to Mr. Fanroy, but it's too late for her to ask. She hopes Joey is in one of her classes. She really likes him.

The tremendous noise emanating from the halls sounds like bedlam. Gail decides it may be best to avoid venturing out just yet. She looks for a piece of chalk to write her name on the small strip of blackboard space, but there is none. She feels her palms begin to sweat as anxiety builds. She hopes she can pull herself together soon, before the students arrive. She jumps when she hears the knock at her door.

"Oh dear, they're here!" she exclaims under her breath. Gail remains suspended in a state of frozen silence for seconds. Finally, she grabs both ends of her desk and manages, somehow, to respond.

"Come in," she whispers. Realizing that the students could not possibly have heard her, she repeats herself. "Come on in, please!" Just as the door begins to open the bell sounds again. The loud buzzer catches Gail off guard. She jumps up with a start, knocking her Teacher Handbook and course outlines to the floor.

"Good morning, Miss Simmons!" Mrs. Easley says. She automatically begins to help Gail to retrieve the books from the floor. "I'm sorry if I startled you. I didn't know if you had made it OK or not. I had not seen you today, so I thought I'd better check to make sure you will be ready to subdivide the A.P. class right after homeroom this morning."

"Oh, yes," Gail answers, "that will be just fine." She is so happy to see Mrs. Easley that, at this moment, she will agree to almost anything. "I've been waiting for my students to come in, but I haven't seen any yet."

"Oh, no. You won't see any students for at least an hour or so. All students are in homeroom now, and you don't have a homeroom. Neither do I. That's the only advantage you derive from being a latecomer. All of the homerooms had already been assigned before you arrived, so you missed out on that one. The reason I don't have a homeroom is because I'm a department chair. None of the department chairs do. Of course, we do not get any remuneration for all the extra work that we do so the administration tries to give us some free time during the day to make up for it. All department chairs are also given the longest period of the day for planning. That's the fifth period, which also serves as lunch period for everyone. When is your planning period, Gail?"

"I believe it's second period." She looks at the form Cheryl had given her yesterday. "Yes, I plan right after my A.P. class." Several sheets fall to the floor as she speaks. "Wow, this is just what I have been needing all morning. The clock schedule! Mrs. Rossman must have given them to us on yesterday."

"Yes, it would be very unusual for Mrs. Rossman to leave out anything that you will need for today. I see you also have a copy of the lunch schedule which you will need at the fifth period today," Mrs. Easley reminds her.

"But we won't see our fifth period students today, will we? Aren't the students leaving at ten o'clock today?" Gail asks, with a plea in her voice.

"I'm afraid not, Gail." Mrs. Easley's voice softens. "You see, because of the budget cuts and the fact that the state legislature has added another instructional day to the school calendar, the School Board took away the half day for students. This year students will be here for a full day from the very beginning. We are all quite upset about it, but there is nothing we can do. The public feels it's a waste to send students to school for a half day, when it will cost just as much to keep them the whole day. But you and I both know that the people making these decisions haven't set a foot in a school building in the last twenty or thirty years!"

"But let me get off my soap box," Mrs. Easley says. "Is there anything else you need to know about today's schedule?"

"No, I don't think so. I could use a piece of chalk, though."

"You poor dear. Let me get you some supplies. I've been going on about having lost a few hours of planning time and had not even checked to see if you have all the supplies you will need. You have to overlook old-timers like myself. How soon we forget how it was when we were just beginning. Come on, let's go to my room and raid the supply cabinet."

As they proceed down the hall, Gail wonders how Mrs. Easley manages to keep the vast array of information and small details in her head. The lady is like a walking encyclopedia. She talks incessantly, but every morsel is purposeful and intended to enlighten.

Gail leaves Mrs. Easley's room with not only a box of chalk, but a blackboard eraser, ink pens, pencils, notebook paper, copy paper, ink cartridges, a stapler, staples, paper clips, rubber bands, and thumb tacks. The supply cabinet in Mrs. Easley's room reminds Gail of a teacher supply store. Gail also recognizes the fact that Mrs. Easley is one of the haves and she is one of the have nots. Gail is reminded of what her sister told her about having to pay her dues, so none of what she has experienced so far has dampened her mood. Now that she has some supplies, she feels much more excited about the prospect of meeting her students.

It is 9:00 o'clock before students are dismissed from their homeroom and allowed to report to first period class. Dr. Reed, whose voice has been heard all morning, dictates the abbreviated schedule for the rest of the day and admonishes all teachers to adhere to it strictly. Gail takes one last look at the name she has written on the blackboard before she scurries to Mrs. Easley's room. It has been so long since she has written on a blackboard, she can't seem to write straight anymore.

Her heart is pounding by the time she walks into Mrs. Easley's room to meet the A.P. students. Mrs. Easley is talking to them as she arrives. "I am assuming you are familiar with all ten of the novels which appear on your reading list which you took home for the summer. If you have not read them, I would suggest that you drop this course immediately." She does not spare the students any pain or embarrassment. She makes it perfectly clear that much will be expected of them during the year. Gail notices several students with grimaces on their faces as Mrs. Easley continues.

Mrs. Easley turns toward Gail. "Miss Simmons, as you can see, we have quite a large class here. I have thirty-five desks in this room and they are all taken, yet we still have ten students who are standing against the walls. Before we split this group, I want to make sure that these students are serious about staying in A.P. This is a college-level course for which they can receive college credit once they successfully pass the Advanced Placement Test. But, they must understand the importance of making a commitment to write an analytical essay every night as well as keep up with all the reading requirements of this course. Now, I will ask the question one more time. Is there anyone who has neglected to read the ten novels assigned during the summer? If you know you have not read those novels, please be kind enough to drop this class now!"

There is a long pause during which time Mrs. Easley pivots from one foot to the next with her hands perched on her hips, waiting for someone to break the silence. She looks in each students' eyes as if she can discern which one has not read those novels. Gail feels a bit sorry for them as they sit under the gaze of Mrs. Easley's piercing stare. No one moves, and Gail understands why. Gail wonders where she might be able to get her hands on a copy of that reading list.

"Does this mean I am going to have to read ten novels in order to work with this class?" she wonders. "Oh, boy," she sighs, under her breath, "this is going to be a nightmare."

"Now that this little detail has been taken care of and we know that no one has signed up for the wrong class, we are ready to subdivide this group," Mrs. Easley continues. "As you know, there is no way we can possibly work together and accomplish all that we need to accomplish this year as large as we are. So, at least twenty of you will need to go with Miss Simmons, who will be teaching this course in room 239. Miss Simons is new at Melrose this year, but she is going to be just as tough as I am. We are going to work very closely so that we will all cover the material. Now, if there are no questions, I need twenty of you to voluntarily go with Miss Simmons." No one moves. "If enough of you do not volunteer, you will be drafted."

Suddenly, and without warning, a surge of students starts moving toward the door. Once one student makes the first move, they converge like lava from a volcano. Gail moves to the front of the group, rather oblivious to what is occurring. It is not until she reaches her small room that she realizes all twenty-four desks in her room are filled and students are still pouring in. "Wait!" she announces nervously. "Something is wrong here. I think I have too many. Didn't Mrs. Easley ask for twenty volunteers?" The thirty-five students look at one another as if Miss Simmons is speaking a foreign language.

Suddenly a hand is raised. "Well, I think the students who have seats should be allowed to stay and those who don't have seats should go back to Mrs. Easley," a petite redhead suggests.

"We're going to do better than that," Cheryl Rossman announces unexpectedly. She suddenly appears at the doorway as she does so many other times. Somehow she seems to appear just at the right time. She doesn't get in the teachers' way and one of her primary concerns is that classes not be interrupted; yet, she is there when they need her. "Since there are four rows of seats in this room, with a total of six desks in each row, I will arbitrarily take one person from each row and ask that you report back to Mrs. Easley, along with all of you who are still standing. Come on, let's move." Groans can be heard from quite a distance as fourteen students move back in the direction of Mrs. Easley's room.

Cheryl returns just long enough to apologize to Gail for having arrived much later than she had intended. She explains the multitude of problems that have surfaced relative to registration, and Gail certainly understands. Cheryl then asks if Gail needs anything or has any questions. As soon as Gail responds, Cheryl disappears just as ominously as she appeared.

As Cheryl closes the door and Gail realizes that she is alone with those twenty students, her palms begin to sweat again. She fidgets with the Teacher Handbook on her desk and looks up at the clock. It is 9:35. Gail has forgotten what time Dr, Reed said the period would end. "Oh, gee," she thinks to herself. "Why didn't I think to write those times down?" A hand is raised in the back.

"Yes?" she asks.

"Are you going to give us a syllabus so we will know what to expect for the semester?" the student asks.

"We---ll," she begins hesitantly. "I'm sure I will at some point. Maybe tomorrow." She doesn't mean to say that, but it's out before she realizes. She wants to retract that statement, but she doesn't really know how. What she does know is that there is no way she will have a syllabus prepared by tomorrow, unless of course, she stays up all night. As she sees another hand go up, she unconsciously moves close to the wall behind her desk.

"What are we going to do today?" the boy with glasses asks. Gail looks at the student and knows right away that the student is a genius. He reminds her of Larry Lightfoot who graduated as valedictorian of her high school class. It all fits; the dark shaggy hair almost hanging into his eyes; the way he holds his head straight and stiff; the way his eyes move swiftly from one area of the room to the next, analyzing and synthesizing.

"Nothing, Dexter!" a voice from the back replies. "The bell rings in two seconds." In exactly two seconds the loud buzz that startled Gail a few hours earlier comes as the most welcome sound she has ever heard.

Gail knows for certain that she never again wants to feel the sense of helplessness that she felt during the last class period. Since the second period has been designated as her planning time, she decides to ask Mrs. Easley for help so that she will know what to do for the remainder of the day. When she peers through the small rectangular glass window of Mrs. Easley's classroom door, however, and sees the room filled with students, she immediately withdraws. There is no way she is going inside that room. When she feels the sense of helplessness returning, she decides to find Cheryl.

The atmosphere in Cheryl's office differs from that in the main building. It is unusually quiet. Instead of the constant sound of students' voices, typewriters and copiers seem to work incessantly. Customized draperies frame the windows. The entire building, except for the science labs, is carpeted. Gail remembers having been told that Cheryl moved her entire office staff into an adjoining building and created a curriculum center when overcrowding necessitated the relocating of some math and science classes.

The reception area of the Curriculum Center is filled with students and parents. They are relatively quiet, but appear somewhat impatient and weary. Some are seated, while others are standing in a line which leads to an open office door. Gail looks for Cheryl's name above one of the doors but doesn't see it. Suddenly the line inches forward and the name becomes visible. Unwilling to believe that all of these people could be waiting to see Cheryl Rossman, Gail moves up to the office door and peers through the crowd.

Cheryl is seated at a long conference table explaining to a group of students why her request for a schedule change must be honored. "The School Board has established certain quotas for class size," Cheryl explains. "Whenever a class exceeds that quota, we must correct the situation. I realize this change is difficult for you to make, but I would certainly appreciate your cooperation." Cheryl never looks up long enough to notice Gail.

She turns and walks slowly back to room 239. Gail tries to think of someone else she can go to for help, but can think of no one. Just as she opens her classroom door the bell buzzes for second period to end. "Mr. Clinard," she whispers to herself. "That's who I can talk to. But, no, that won't work. He has to evaluate me. I'd better not give him any reason to question my capabilities. Besides, we haven't even met yet. He doesn't know I'm here." Feeling lonely and helpless, Gail lets out a long, slow sigh. Suddenly the door swings open.

"Hi," a soft, timid voice whispers. The little girl looks at her schedule card reflectively. "Are you Miss Simmons?"

"Yes," Gail answers.

"Good. Then, I'm in the right place. I've been getting lost all morning. This is my first year here, and I don't know where all the rooms are," the little girl confesses.

"This is my first year here, too," Gail volunteers.

Joey Miller enters the room, smiling crookedly, "Hi, Miss Simmons. Do you remember me?" he asks.

"Of course I remember you, Joey," Gail remarks. "Are you signed up for this class?"

"No ma'am," Joey answers. "I'm assigned to you fifth period for Career Education. Careers Exploration is what they really call it. Are we going to be writing an essay about summer vacation?" Joey inquires.

"Of course!" Gail says to herself. "We used to do that when I was in school. Why hadn't I thought of it? That's what we will do for the rest of the day!"

"How did you guess, Joey? Don't you think that will be fun?"

Thought Questions

Chapter 3 – An Awakening

1. In what way's do Gail's expectations of the first day of school not match reality?

2. What impact is a misalignment of expectations and reality likely to have on a new teacher?

3. How would you describe the first day of school for Gail? Smooth? Rocky? What could have made her first day better? How could it have been made worse?

Chapter 4

AUTUMN

"Sis," Gail begins as she talks to her older sister, Rosie, on the telephone later that evening, "I don't know what to do exactly about this A.P. class. I would like to teach it, but it may be a bit too much for me right now."

"Gail, have I not told you that I would help you? You can do it. I know you can do it. It's just going to be the most rewarding thing you have ever done," Rosie promises.

"I know you've told me that but I have all of these other classes to prepare for, too." Gail switches to the pleading voice that she has used on her sister many times before. "Even Mrs. Rossman asked me today if I would consider switching the A.P. class for another freshman English class in order to reduce my preparations. She realizes how difficult this is going to be."

"Let me explain to you what's really happening with Cheryl Rossman," Gail's sister retorts in her instructive tone. "Cheryl Rossman is probably receiving complaints from other members of that English department about a newcomer like you being assigned that class. I am sure she is. To have been assigned students of that caliber your first year is unheard of. And I am willing to bet money that your schedule is being challenged. I know if I were working at that school I would challenge it. There is no other explanation for it. She is trying to figure out a diplomatic way to get herself out of hot water. I know those teachers who have taught there for a while are furious. No! You hang in there, Gail, and let her sweat it because if you ever give that class up, you will never get it back!"

"Well," Gail attempts to explain. "It did seem that Mrs. Rossman was a bit surprised when Dr. Reed offered me that class during my interview. I don't think she felt it was a good idea, but it was too late. He had already offered it to me."

"Well, you just have to show her what you can do," Rosie replies. "Now the first thing I am going to do is get you a copy of the syllabus we use for A.P. at my school. I will also ask our teacher to call you and give you some pointers. In fact, you may want to follow his curriculum. He's supposed to be the best A.P. teacher in the system or he wouldn't be at the magnet school. So, don't you worry about a thing, little sister. We're going to establish a precedent. We Simmons are known for that, right? Look at Mom, Dad, and myself. We are natural-born teachers. If we can't get the job done in the classroom, no one can. So don't you start doubting yourself, Gail. A Simmons never quits!" As usual, Gail's sister is very convincing. She hasn't won a single argument with her in the last thirty years.

Gail decides to take Rosie's advice. Early the next morning she tells Cheryl that she has decided she definitely wants to keep the A.P. class.

"That's fine, Gail," Cheryl assures her. "If you decide to change your mind later on, just let me know. My concern is that you're new at this and I hate to see you struggle with four preparations. I feel that taking the freshman honors English class will be a reasonable swap because you will still be working with high achievers; yet the amount of material covered and the complexity of the material will be lessened. You will also be able to use the same textbook for the freshman honors group as the freshman standard group that you are already assigned at the third period. The only difference in the two groups is that you move at a more rapid pace with the honors level and assign more writing. But it is entirely up to you. I simply offer this as a suggestion." Gail feels that Cheryl is sincere, yet she trusts her sister explicitly.

For the next two weeks, Gail spends an enormous amount of time preparing for her classes. She is determined to never feel the sense of helplessness that she felt on the first day of school. She finds herself engaged in this process from dawn to dusk and well beyond. Typically, Gail arrives home by 3:00 p.m., after having spent some time organizing her desk for the next day. She eats a light snack when she comes in and immediately begins to prepare for the A.P. class. The reading seems endless and the weekly essays are very time consuming assignments to grade. She tries assigning a daily essay as Mrs. Easley's syllabus dictates but finds it impossible to adhere to that schedule. She witnesses the mound of papers on her small kitchen table grow to a foot high and decides she has to function differently from Mrs. Easley.

Usually by 6:00 p.m. Gail can be found still seated at the kitchen table. But three hours later, she is slumped over an open literature book or a stack of papers, sound asleep. Drained of her energy reservoir, she crawls into bed when she awakens at approximately 9:00 p.m. By then, her back and neck feel as if the services of a chiropractor are needed. Gail sets her alarm for 3:00 a.m., knowing that she must finish making preparations for the A.P. class. She doesn't attempt to plan for her other classes until second period, after the A.P. class ends. That class must be her priority. She has a point to prove. When Gail rises at 3:00 a.m., every joint aches as she sits rigidly at her kitchen table. She and her kitchen table have become companions; they've bonded like an old lady and her easy chair.

At the end of Gail's first two weeks at Melrose, Cheryl calls her in for an interview as a part of the research project she spoke to the newcomers about earlier. Gail is somewhat nervous when she reports for that first interview.

She does not know what to expect exactly. Cheryl explains the purposes of her research again and makes a special effort to help Gail to relax. She once again asks Gail to explain why she decided to leave her sales position at the publishing company in order to teach full time. Cheryl then asks Gail what her experience has been like for the past two weeks.

"Well, I've definitely had ups and downs," Gail begins rather hesitantly. "I think it would be very nice. . . I mean, I know it's impossible, really, but, if people knew six months ahead of time that they were going to be hired". . . Cheryl waits patiently for Gail to finish her thought. "I guess some people . . . you just need so much time to prepare." Gail seems exasperated as she finishes.

Cheryl tries to paraphrase Gail's comments and bring things into perspective. "That's true. And for you, that's the missing link right now. The fact is that you have not had adequate time to prepare. Am I right?"

"Uh-huh," Gail responds softly. "And then, just being a new teacher. Not just here at Melrose, but not having a backlog of things to fall back on."

"Right," Cheryl agrees.

"So, it's just going from scratch every way you look at it," Gail explains.

"That's very true," Cheryl agrees. "I was thinking that you had taught before for an extended period of time, but you really have not."

"No," Gail assures her. "Not in a permanent capacity."

"So, you are brand new to the field." Cheryl repeats for emphasis. "Tell me about your schedule, now." Cheryl has interviewed four other participants and asks the question both for clarification and to help Gail to relax and share information with her. "Tell me about your classes. You've got one A.P. class. . ."

"Yeah," Gail interrupts. "A.P. is first period and then planning, which is nice because I can get everything for the A.P. prepared the previous night and then use my planning time to get everything ready for the rest of the day. Because A.P. class is so totally different from everything else."

"Yeah. Right. It is."

"Then," Gail continues, "Third, I've got the little freshmen." She laughs when she mentions this group. "The standard English class;" she continues, "I like them. They're a good class. I mean,. . . there are one or two that give me a problem sometime, but basically they're a pretty good class. And then, fourth period is my first eleventh grade proficiency English class. And it's just a wild class!" Her voice becomes quite animated as she continues, "Career Education is next. I change rooms to go to Career Education, which is hard. I didn't think about that at first, but changing rooms is really hard. And there are so many of them! There are 35 of them! Well, I've dropped a couple in the last few days. It's down to 33 now. And then I go back to my room at sixth period for my second proficiency English class. And it's so strange because, one day the fourth period class will be good; the next day they will be horrible. Then I will go in expecting sixth period to be bad and they will be good. There's no predicting what they're going to do."

Gail laughs nervously as she continues, "Now, I do feel like I'm getting a better grasp on all of them."

"I see."

"Yesterday, I had to put fourth period in a new seating arrangement and it was much better today," Gail adds.

"Isn't that interesting?" Cheryl remarks.

"Uh--huh. Much better. I had one of them absent. It would have made a difference probably, if he had been there. But. They are doing a lot better now," Gail explains.

Cheryl probes for more. "So you think the teaching situation is steadily improving.....your teaching situation?"

"Yes."

"Okay." Cheryl rephrases the question. "And whatever problems you have, the situation is salvageable?"

"Uh-huh . . . uh-huh,"

"Okay. All right," Cheryl says cautiously.

"Most definitely!" Gail insists. "First period, you know, I was a little scared about it at first because I didn't want to blow it. But I think that's going to be fine," Gail insists.

"I've still got to get some ideas about helping them with their writing. Because I thought, I really expected that they would write a lot and I would make some suggestions on maybe the content. But some of them need things more basic than the content."

"Like mechanics and grammar," Cheryl suggests.

"Yes," Gail responds, "but more advanced mechanics than my ninth, tenth, and eleventh graders."

"Well. That's true." Cheryl agrees.

"So," Gail continues, "I need some kind of help with teaching writing."

"Yes," Cheryl says with delight. "Mrs. Easley can certainly help you with that. There is a writing workshop that you probably need to attend this summer...."

"Yeah, she's told me about it," Gail interrupts.

Cheryl continues, obviously enjoying this opportunity to nurture Gail along. "There is also a book that you may want to look at. You will find that I try to provide some flexibility in terms of curriculum." She moves to the bookshelf behind her desk which contains a vast array of textbooks.

"I see," Gail says with interest.

"This is the twelfth grade book that I want you to review," Cheryl explains. "See, this is composition and writing. It's a pilot that we did last year. The teachers really liked the book, but it was not our adoption."

"This book concentrates entirely on writing," Cheryl emphasizes. "Okay. There is grammar and writing. Look at how this is organized and see if this will be a better resource for you."

"Un-huh. I really don't have much in the way of resources."

"I will certainly allow you to use it. Now, this is a teacher's edition. ., ."

"Oh, that's great! You mean there is a teacher's edition?"

"Yes. What you may want to do with this is see how the teacher's edition is done so that you will know if it's going to give you the ideas and explanations that you need. . .,"

"Un-huh." Gail looks at the book closely.

Cheryl continues, "And if it will get at the problems that you're finding your students have."

"Okay. That's what I recommend with the situation you're describing. This is an excellent tool for strengthening students' writing skills."

"Oh great! Because that's what they need. That's what they need on the A.P. test."

"Yes, it is!" Cheryl agrees. Now, I am sure we have enough of these for all of your students. It's an excellent resource for teaching writing skills."

"Okay, now," Cheryl reminds her, "this is one of the advantages of working with me on this research project. You do get a few extras every now and then. Otherwise, you more than likely wouldn't have had a chance to tell me how you felt about that A.P. group."

"That's true," Gail agrees. "It's odd, too, because we have just gone into all of these pieces of great literature and, you know, we are doing all of these great plays, like the *Iliad* and the *Odyssey.*"

"Yes."

"I just realized that probably what I need," Gail continues, "is a teacher's edition or a study guide on all of these books. And my sister is a teacher. She suggested that I get a copy from the Teacher Center."

"Yeah. Right. I would think that a study guide would certainly be beneficial. And you may want to check some of the bookstores this weekend."

"Well, I've been doing some checking." Gail has become more relaxed, now. "And it helps. I've gotten some different things. But, it's like I'm reading it and then I, you know, think it would be nice to get something that you learn from. Like a teaching guide." She sighs rather pensively, as if she is groping for the answer. "If there is such a thing, now. I don't know."

"I would certainly think so," Cheryl suggests.

"Somewhere." Gail continues to sigh,

"But, at this point," Cheryl continues "you're having to grab everything; absorb it all so you can be totally prepared for the students. And that's tough."

"It's tough!" Gail reiterates. "It's that reading. Now, I told them that I'm reading these works again and I'm reading them right along with you. If I can do it, you can, too." There is a long pause. Gail waits for an answer, while Cheryl waits for more information, more detail regarding those events which form the tapestry of Gail's experience as a newcomer to Melrose.

Gail leaves her first interview feeling that she has a tough challenge ahead but determined in her resolve to meet that challenge. Her first attempt at meeting the challenge is to work toward improving the writing skills of her A.P. students. On Monday morning of her third week, she approaches Mrs. Easley about her concerns.

"Well," Mrs. Easley remarks. "I have no problem at all in teaching you what I know about writing skills instruction. Why don't we put our classes together and team teach a unit on writing? I will explain to you what we are going to do and then you can watch me and simply model my behavior. And, of course, I will be there to assist you in any way that I can."

"Oh, great! When can we begin?"

"Where are you? Have you finished the *Iliad* and the *Odyssey*?" Mrs. Easley asks.

Gail hesitates. "No. I'm afraid we are still on the *Iliad* and the *Odyssey*."

"Well, that's fine. We are discussing *Wuthering Heights*, now. But, we can go back to the *Iliad* and the *Odyssey* for a few days and do a couple of analytical writings on some new topics, so don't concern yourself with that. I will simply hold them responsible for reading *Wuthering Heights* outside of class until we finish our writing seminar. Will you be ready to start on Wednesday?"

"I will be ready, just any time."

"Then tell your students that day after tomorrow we will be meeting in the Curriculum Center in the large lecture hall. We can arrange the desks in circles to facilitate their working in groups. I will call Mrs. Rossman right now to make sure the lecture hall will be available." Mrs. Easley's expertise is unquestionable, and Gail feels fortunate to have this golden opportunity to work in the same classroom with her.

Having successfully set that plan into motion, Gail gains renewed confidence. Having relieved some of the pressure relating to the A.P. students, she begins to take a closer look at her other classes and concludes that they are getting out of control. The students are loud and there are so many constant interruptions that she has little time to think. The two proficiency English classes are definitely loud and disruptive, but because there are only fifteen students in each class she finds the situation tolerable. Her worst class appears to be the Career Education class she teaches in room 204, the class of 33.

Gail did not realize it was possible for a class to mushroom so quickly. She began with twelve students enrolled, but as the weeks have come and gone, more and more students have been added. She is forced to move to another room in order to accommodate the students because her room seats only twenty-four. Luckily for Gail, the teacher she replaced at Ambrosia High School ten years ago is now working at Melrose. Since Mrs. Berry does not have a fifth period class, Gail feels comfortable asking her if she can meet the career education class in her room. During her third week at Melrose, Gail decides to talk to Wilma Berry about this class.

"Wilma, do you have a moment to talk to me about a little problem I have?" she asks rather apologetically.

"I sure do, Gail. What can I help you with?" Wilma's manner exudes warmth and genuine concern.

"I know this may sound trivial, but my Career Education class has become a bit tough to handle," Gail explains.

"Well, that's not surprising in view of the fact that the class is so large. Has Mrs. Rossman said anything to you about reducing it?"

"Yes, she has. She was able to move only two students."

"Well, why don't you tell me what appears to be happening, dear." Wilma moves closer to Gail in an effort to be more reassuring,

"Well…, it's just that they seem to have so much energy. They're all over the place, and I can't seem to keep up with them," Gail confesses. "It gets really bad when we go to lunch. Half of them don't come back on time, and when they come back late they always use the excuse that they were assigned to tray duty. I don't know what tray duty is, but shouldn't they have a note when they are assigned to tray duty?"

"Yes, they should have a note when they are assigned tray duty. And you have every right to request one." Wilma states emphatically.

"What exactly is tray duty?"

"Students are assigned tray duty as punishment for some infraction. It's an alternative that some of our principals use to avoid sending students home on suspension, which is all well and good. But, my point is that they should not be assigned tray duty at a time when they should be in your class. The way I understand it, the students pick up trays only during the period of time when they are scheduled to be in the cafeteria. When their lunch period ends, they are supposed to check with their principal and report back to class with a clearance note. Is this not happening?"

"Well, I really have not made an issue of it. When they say they have been assigned tray duty I have just taken their word for it. I didn't know what to do, to be perfectly honest. I also have problems keeping up with them when we first go to lunch. I found a note in my mailbox the other day reminding me that I'm supposed to escort my students to the cafeteria and pick them up from the cafeteria. I have tried, but a soon as we leave this room, they scatter. I honestly don't know if they report to the cafeteria or not. I hope this doesn't get me into trouble. That note sounded pretty serious."

"You know, I've heard several people mention that note. I didn't get one, because I don't have a class in the fifth period. But several people are irritated at the tone of the memo. Dr. Johnson sent that memo only because he is the assistant principal in charge of the cafeteria. I doubt very seriously if he's even aware of who's not following the procedure. I know most of the teachers in this school don't escort their students to lunch and back because it is simply too embarrassing for these students. It's too bad the principals don't realize how senseless that is. But, getting back to your group. Why don't you ask Mr. Clinard to sit in on that class and see if that helps?" Wilma suggests.

"I really didn't want to create a problem."

"You will not be creating a problem, I assure you. Mr. Clinard is your principal and he is very understanding. He will be more than happy to help you with that class. Why don't you just go by and talk to him about it right after school today?" I guarantee you he will get some of those characters straightened out, because most of those students are seniors anyway. I know them. They are good kids, but I think they may be trying to take advantage of the fact that you're new to Melrose and haven't learned all the games they play yet. Isn't Joey Miller in that class?"

"Yes, he is. And Joey is an absolute joy. He doesn't create a problem at all. In fact, I sometimes feel badly about his being in there. He always wants to help. He is such a special child."

"Yes," Wilma agrees. "Joey is a good role model for the other students. He's a member of the Student Government Association, too, so he's supposed to be a good role model. If there are students creating a problem in that class, though, Mr. Clinard needs to know. He can certainly tell you who has been delayed because of tray duty." Wilma sounds very convincing.

"It certainly won't hurt to just talk to him, will it?"

"No, Gail. It certainly will not. Now, is there anything else I can help you with?"

"Yes, one more thing. I understand we are supposed to issue textbooks tomorrow. Can you tell me what the procedures are?"

"I will be happy to."

By the time Wilma explains the textbook procedures to Gail, it is time for her to report to the cafeteria to pick up her students. Only five or six of the thirty-three students bother to come when she dutifully stands at her post to summon them. Joey Miller is always a member of that group. Today she decides to wait five minutes longer to see if more students will report. While she waves her arms trying to see if she can get the attention of a few more students, she feels a light tap on her shoulder. Gail wheels around expecting to see one of her playful students.

"Pardon me," the petite stranger replies. "Can you tell me how to get to the main office from here? Today is my first day, and I haven't learned my way around yet."

"Sure. The main office is directly down those steps to your left. Wait." Gail remembers how easy it is to get lost in a large building such as this one. "Joey, we have a new student who needs to go to the main office. Will you take her down there while we're waiting for the rest of the class? Oh, I'm sorry. I didn't get your name. My name is Gail Simmons. I teach English in the room right around the corner from here. What grade are you in?"

"I'm a new teacher. I was just hired on yesterday to teach math. My name is Laura Perkins."

"I apologize," Gail says. "You look so young, I just knew you were a student. What room will you be in? I'd like to help you get settled."

"Well," Laura says, "that's just the problem. I don't have a classroom of my own. I migrate from one room to another all day. The first period I'm on the second floor, but I'm on the first floor for the rest of the day. I move around to five different rooms."

"Oh, dear. That's terrible. Is there any likelihood that you will be getting a room of your own, soon?"

"I doubt it. All of my students were pulled from overcrowded classes the first week of school and given to a substitute. The substitute quit after three days and then another one came and stayed a week. The third substitute left on Friday. There's no room available, because this is a new position they didn't know they would need. Dr. Reed said I would probably be able to get a room next year. The classes are really in a mess and the students are very upset. They keep asking me when I'm going to leave." Laura smiles rather nervously and looks toward the stairway.

"I'll take you down to the main office now if you're ready," Joey volunteers.

"Yes, I had better get on down there so I can get back up here within ten minutes. I don't believe I'll have time to eat anything today." Laura peers at her watch as Joey escorts her down to the main office.

Gail wonders how she would feel if she were just coming aboard three weeks into the school year. She doesn't think she could survive it. She realizes, now, how fortunate she is to have at least been hired before the first day of school.

"I've accomplished a lot in three weeks," she thinks. "Things could be much worse. If I had it all to do over again, though, I don't know if I would do it." She is lost in her own thoughts when Joey bounces back up the steps.

"I'm back, Miss Simmons," Joey says with his usual grin. "That new teacher is really going to be busy. Guess what she told me when we were on the way down stairs?" Joey asks.

"What's that?" Gail says, still thinking about the struggle of the last three weeks.

"She's our new sponsor for the school newspaper and yearbook. I told her I would help her, though," Joey adds.

Thought Questions

Chapter 4 – Autumn

1. **How would you define Joey Miller's role in the organization?**

2. **Define Wilma Berry's role.**

3. **Define Gail's sister's role.**

4. **What do you feel should be Gail's next steps, at this point?**

Chapter 5

THE WINTER

In the gymnasium, also known as the Rose Garden, two thousand students sway, chant, clap, and stomp their feet. Twelve female students, petite and immensely attractive, command the audience. They dance around the floor in red, white and blue costume; their movements fast and calculated; their gaze all encompassing; their voices electric. Seated on the floor are sixteen well-built, male students, also attired in red, white, and blue uniforms. They do not cheer. Instead they sit quietly as if spellbound by goddesses. They wait patiently to receive their power, prestige, and confidence from the cheering crowd. Several male teachers stand high above the cheering crowd trying desperately to anticipate events and squelch any signs of unrest or absence of 'esprit de corps.'

Like uninvited guests, many teachers stand sandwiched in the doorways cautiously peering into the faces of the cheering crowd. Gail wonders if they will be able to make a clean getaway if things get out of control. When the cheering reaches its peak, several walk out into the lobby momentarily with fingers jammed in their ears. But what appears to be wild chaos is a well-orchestrated celebration; a rallying point for the Melrose school and community. The beginning cheers of the pep rally are reminiscent of an old-fashioned roll call:

Cheerleaders: Is the gang all here?
Audience: Yeah! Yeah!
Cheerleaders: Are you ready to cheer?
Audience: Yeah! Yeah!
Cheerleaders: Then, what you gonna do?
Answer in Unison: Yeah! Yeah! We gonna yell like a fool!

Then, get it together. Let's go!
Come on, Roses! Let's go!
Come on Roses! Let's go!

The walls appear to rivet when the final cheer, led by Dr. Reed himself, echoes through the air:

Dr. Reed: Who we gonna beat?
Answer: Wingate!!
Dr. Reed: Who we gonna beat?
Answer: Wingate!!
Dr. Reed: I can't hear you!
Answer: Wingate!!!
Dr. Reed: I can't hear you!
Answer: Wingate!!!!

Before the pep rally reaches its frenzied conclusion, Dr. Reed motions for four teachers to position themselves in the middle of the gymnasium floor in preparation for the spirit-stick competition. Their job is to see which group of students can cheer the loudest and with the greatest enthusiasm. As Dr. Reed waves the red, white, and blue spirit stick high in the air, the students take turns cheering for the Roses. They cheer by grade levels, the ninth graders first and the seniors last. Each grade level attempts to out cheer the other. Their shrill voices can be heard from one end of the building to the other. When all four grade levels have cheered, Dr. Reed momentarily confers with the four teachers for the decisive vote.

Absolute quiet surrounds the gymnasium as everyone awaits Dr. Reed's announcement. As the four judges move back toward the doorway, Dr. Reed methodically moves to the middle of the gym floor with the spirit stick hoisted high in the air and announces, "The winner of the spirit stick competition for this week and the class with the most school spirit is the senior class!" A throng of well-intentioned, exuberant seniors rushes to the floor to accept their prized spirit stick and almost tramples Dr. Reed in the process. Nonetheless, the sixteen young men still seated in one corner of the gymnasium floor are convinced of success at tonight's football game against their number one rival, Wingate High.

Movement back to class begins almost immediately after Dr. Reed announces the winning group. All groups, except the seniors, move rather quietly. The seniors continue to celebrate with shouts of victory and superiority.

"We're number one! We're number one!" They shout in unison.

"Miss Simmons," Mrs. Easely inquires, "how did you like your first pep rally?"

"It was quite an event." Gail answers, pleased to know that Mrs. Easley is walking beside her. "Will we have a pep rally every Friday?"

"No. Not usually. Dr. Reed just seems to call for them when the spirit hits him. He's quite a sports enthusiast. He and the cheerleaders usually decide, after conferring with the coaches."

Mrs. Easley pauses momentarily as she climbs the last stairwell, then continues. "You will find that there are two schools of thought relative to the usefulness of pep rallies, and in all honesty there are pros and cons on both sides of the issue of whether to have or not to have pep rallies. Some claim they are a complete waste of valuable instructional time, while others emphasize the benefits derived from providing an avenue through which students can act out in constructive ways. Dr. Reed's philosophy is that pep rallies provide the one opportunity for the total school and community to work toward a common goal – that of defeating a common rival. To Dr. Reed, a school without a rallying point is a school headed for failure."

"And what about you?" Gail inquires.

"Well, I'm from the old school of thought. The pep rally is a necessary evil we have to contend with in order to placate the coaches and keep ticket sales high. I don't let pep rallies bother me, one way or the other. I have learned to roll with the punches. I just make sure I have so much work for the kids to do after the pep rally that they don't have time to dwell on it."

Gail has learned that when Mrs. Easley tilts her chin upward and peers from underneath her glasses, she is finished with that subject. She retreats to her classroom.

Gail smiles to herself as she sticks a thumbtack in the last letter she has to mount to complete her bulletin board on careers. She stands back and takes one last look to see if all the letters are straight and centered. "Boy," she mutters under her breath, "that's not so bad. At least this will let Mr. Clinard know that I'm really interested in this class. I do hope everything goes well." She sighs deeply as she rehearses in her mind each step that she will take today.

"Let's see, is this the period I'm supposed to evaluate you?" Mr. Clinard asks.

"Yes, it is," Gail replies, her voice cracking slightly.

"I just wanted to make sure," he says, politely. "Sometimes I tend to get things mixed up, especially when it comes to new folks." He holds a pad and pen in his right hand and keeps the other one deeply embedded in his pocket. His pants always seem to hang below a bulging stomach, protruding from a jacket that seems too small.

"I wanted to get here before the bell sounded so I wouldn't come in and disturb you," he explains. Gail notices that he never looks her directly in the eye, but squints. She wonders if he has spent a lot of time working in the sun. He removes his left hand from his pocket long enough to wipe his forehead as he takes the last seat in the back corner. Gail was hoping he would at least wait until she had called the roll before he came in.

"Now, Ms. Simmons," Mr. Clinard continues, "what I'm going to do today is a focused evaluation. As I explained to you on yesterday, I will write down on my pad as much as I can of what you and your students say to each other. This way we will have a record of the student and teacher interaction that occurs. After class, you and I will sit down together and go over the log to identify some patterns, and so on. So, don't pay me any attention at all. Just conduct the class as you normally do."

"Hi, Teach!" shouts Mickey Slade in his usual boisterous fashion. "Why you so dressed up, today? I hope this don't mean you expecting us to do some work."

"Slade!"

"Don't get bent out of shape, Ms. Simmons. I was just kidding. I just come by to give you my write-off from yesterday. You said to write it 100 times, right?"

"No, Slade, 500 times," Gail emphasizes. "Yesterday was not the first day you were late coming to class. You were late every day last week, so it's 100 times for each day."

"Aww, gee! C'mon Miss Simmons. Gimme a break. How can you expect me to write something 500 times? Be for real. I thought you and me had a understanding. C'mon," he pleads. "I won't ever be late again. I promise."

The crumpled paper Mickey Slade shoves toward Gail has been folded to form an airplane. She looks at the frayed edges of the paper, which has been torn from a spiral notebook, and notices that the statement has been written exactly 100 times.

"Just this once, Slade," she sighs. "Just this once. But next time you're late to my class I will see that you get suspended." She is surprised that she has used such strong language in dealing with Slade, but she hopes to show Mr. Clinard that she is a strong disciplinarian. Besides, the bell has rung, and it is time to start class. She feels that Mr. Clinard will expect her to start on time. She nervously rearranges things on her desk, deliberately avoiding Mr. Clinard's gaze.

When she gathers up enough nerve to look up, she cannot distinguish one face from another. All the faces have become a blur. She immediately looks back down at her roll book and opens her mouth to call the roll. She calls the first three names and no one answers. Once she is able to focus she notices that only half of her students are present.

"Where is everybody?" She asks, softly.

"They're on the way, Ms. Simmons," says a timid voice from the front row. "You know they're never here on time."

Praying that Mr. Clinard did not hear the last statement, she continues. "OK, class. I need your attention, please." The noise level does not change. She clears her throat and moves in closer to their desks. "Class?" The noise stops. "Please respond when your name is called."

"Bass."

"Present!"

"Booker."

"Right here!"

"Brown." No one answers.

"Brown?"

"She won't be back. Somebody laid her up!" The whole class howls with laughter. Several of the young men exchange handclasps. Gail watches Mr. Clinard's face turn crimson. She feels her stomach muscles tighten.

"Class. Please get quiet so I can finish." Her voice is barely audible above the laughter.

"Burrows."

"Yo! I'm coming in the door!"

"You're late Burrows!" Gail says as she walks to the chalkboard and writes the words: "I will not be late to class. – 500 times." Across from the statement she records Burrows' name. "Your write-off is due tomorrow, Burrows."

"Wait up, Ms. Simmons, you didn't even ask why I'm late. Don't be puttin' my name up there, just 'cause Mr. Clinard is in here. You ain't been

49

writin' names on the board. And, besides, why you making me write-off 500 times? You been telling everybody else to write-off 100 times."

"Yeah!" several students shout in unison.

"Beginning today," Gail warns, "everyone who is late will have to write-off 500 times." Five latecomers emerge in the doorway just as she is explaining the new rule.

"What!?!" they say in unison as their names are written on the blackboard.

"I'm not doing it!"

"Who said that?" Gail asks. No one answers, but at least there is silence. She begins to wonder if she should bother to finish calling the roll. The roll book begins to quiver, so she moves to the stool, sits down and rests the roll book on her lap. She carefully pulls her black skirt down enough to cover her knees as she continues to call the roll.

"Carter."

"Carter?"

"Uh—mmm."

"Wake, up, Carter!" Gail admonishes. "You're supposed to sleep at home."

"Stay off my case!" he snaps. Several giggles can be heard around the room.

"You better wake up, man, Mr. Clinard is back there. You have to catch up on your sleep another day," someone warns. Carter reluctantly raises his head, resting his chin on his elbow. The door slams as six more latecomers enter class. Gail continues to call the roll.

"Miss Simmons, that ain't even right!" Burrows shouts. "You let six people come in later than I was and you goin' let them get away with it? You know that ain't right!"

"I'm planning to put their names on the board, Burrows. Just give me a little time. OK?"

"You better do somethin'. I don't play that!"

"Sounds like a threat to me, Miss Simmons. You goin' let Burrows talk to you that way?" Carter questions. He points an accusing finger at Burrows and laughs. Gail's eyes begin to burn as she tries desperately to control her quivering chin. A buzzer goes off and the metallic sound of one door closing against another can be heard in the corridor.

Dr. Reed's announcement comes next. "We will now have a fire drill!" Students scramble to their feet as Gail breathes a sigh of relief. "Will I ever make it through this?" she wonders to herself as she joins the crowd of faces moving out of the building. She dries her sweaty palms against the side of her soft skirt.

The room smells like a pair of wet sneakers when Gail unlocks it after the fire drill. Since the windows are stationary, she has no recourse but to leave the door ajar so that air can circulate. Once all 33 students arrive, they are packed in like sardines. Gail takes a deep breath and assures herself that everything is going to work out. Mr. Clinard returns and occupies his seat in the far corner of the room.

"So that we will be able to finish our lesson for today, we need to go ahead and get started. I will check the roll later. What we are going to do today is discuss our career choices. I want each of you to tell me what your future career choice is so that we can research it. Are there any questions? Okay, then, who would like to volunteer to go first?"

"I will, Miss Simmons!" Joey Miller states with excitement. "I plan to become a mortician someday." The entire class rocks with laughter. Some students find Joey's career choice distasteful.

"Ugh! Ugh! That sounds like something you would like to do, Joey Miller. I always thought you were some sort of a creep!"

"Wait, now, Billy Burrows, I think that Mortuary Science is a good career choice. What do you intend to become?" Gail asks.

"A drug dealer and a pimp that's what! And I bet I will have a whole lot more money than Joey, and also drive a much bigger car. Now. What ya think about that, Teach?"

Gail feels the knot in the pit of her stomach tighten as she struggles to fight back the tears. She knows the signs. First, the back of her neck becomes hot and by the time the surge of heat reaches her face, the tears come uncontrollably. She fights the tears with every fiber of strength she can muster. Finally, she feels the tears subside. "Oh, God!" she whispers to herself. "Please help me through this."

When she is able to see clearly, she witnesses Billy Burrows standing in the middle of the aisle taking a bow. Anthony Booker and several of his friends are applauding. The rest of the class is riveting with laughter and jeers.

"Sit down, Billy Burrows!" she shouts as forcefully as she can. He immediately complies.

"Seriously, Miss Simmons. Seriously," Billy says, apologetically, "I plan to be a cop."

"I don't know, Billy," she says as she shakes her head in disbelief. As Mr. Clinard gets up to leave, Gail reads total disappointment in his face.

"Miss Simmons, what if you don't know what you want to be?" the timid girl seated on the front row asks.

"You can take a test to determine your aptitude," Gail answers. By now, many of the students are talking to one another about various topics of interest. Gail wonders what she did wrong. Joey Miller, interested in pursuing the subject on career choices, walks up to Gail's desk.

"Miss Simmons, have you met our career counselor, Mr. Pope?" he asks.

"No. Joey, I haven't."

"Well, when I was a freshman he came to my English class and talked to us about careers for a whole week and gave us some kind of test. He may be willing to help us."

"Really, Joey?" Gail asks. "Where do I find him?"

"Write me a note and I'll go tell him you'd like to see him." Joey volunteers.

"Will you write me a note, too, Miss Simmons?" the timid girl on the front row asks. "There may be some films in the library on careers."

"Yeah, let's do that," she says with interest.

She writes their notes through teary eyes and sends them on their way. She closes the door tightly so that the noise from her classroom will not be heard so easily. She feels that the students no longer acknowledge her presence. She wonders what Mr. Clinard will say to her this afternoon.

"Hey, Teach!" Billy Burrows bellows. "Don't forget to write down those other names on the board." Gail breathes a sigh of relief as the bell rings. Just as it rings, a student enters the room with a sealed envelope from Mr. Clinard.

Thought Questions

Chapter 5 – The Winter

1. What do you think is in the envelope from Mr. Clinard?

2. How would you describe the students' behavior?

3. What do you feel Gail could have done to have handled this situation better?

4. If you were Gail, what would you do at this point?

Chapter 6

RAINY DAYS

"Okay," Cheryl begins, "let's look back, if we can. I would like for you to describe what it's been like for the past month. You've been here four weeks now. The last time we talked was two weeks ago. Give me a little bit more detail on what it's been like since the last time we talked."

Gail feels very uncomfortable. She rubs her sweaty palms against her dark brown skirt. "Ummmm. . .it's hard. It's very hard. Just last week I started sleeping again. I've gotten very little sleep for a while. And it just takes so much energy."

"What takes your energy?" Cheryl asks.

Gail lets out a long, slow sigh. "I think that a lot of it is discipline problems. And if I can get those things straightened out. . .just interruptions."

"OK."

"I think if I can get that straightened out, things will go along smoothly."

"Right." Cheryl rests her hand under her chin, listening closely.

"And I was just noticing in that fourth period class today, you get used to it in a way – having more interruptions. And all of a sudden when the interruptions aren't there, you can think."

She and Cheryl both laugh.

"Have you gotten a feel for what it's going to take to keep them at that level of solitude?" Cheryl asks.

"Ummm. . . . No!"

Gail laughs again.

"I don't think I've gotten that yet. I hope. . . I think it will come."

"Yes. Yes, I think so." Cheryl assures her. "We might pursue that sometime. . . . . Just looking at the group and figuring what the group requires in order to function at a lower level of frustration for you."

"I would like that," Gail says. But she wonders if Cheryl knows just how bad things are.

"Okay. All right. What are some of the other things that stand out in your mind about the last four weeks? Are things a little smoother than they were the first couple of weeks?"

"Yes. I think they are. It still comes and goes, I mean ... it's still pretty bad. I guess what I'm saying is, one day I'll expect a class to be one way and they are totally different."

"I see." Cheryl says, attempting to understand. "I see."

"And I can't really determine which way it's going to go."

"Right."

"Well, just the fact that I know them now makes it easier. Because I know who they are. I know how they're doing."

"Later on, you will get a feel for the total group. And you'll know what kinds of activities in which to engage them on a particular day and what types not to engage them in on a particular day," Cheryl explains.

"Ummmmm." Gail really listens closely, now, and wants to hear more. She leans forward in an effort to get closer to Cheryl, who sits on the other side of the almond conference table. She glances uncomfortably at the tape recorder which has been placed between them.

"That's when you really get into the pulse of a classroom ... the culture of the group," Cheryl continues.

"That's interesting."

"Right. And you may decide that there are some activities they can't deal with at all. Although you may have the same lesson plans for the two classes, you may decide that you have to organize differently for one particular group than you have to do for the other."

Gail's thoughts go back to the career education class. She feels the intense warmth that always precedes the tears.

Cheryl continues, "For instance, in one group, you may be able to review for a spelling test by having a spelling bee. With the other group, you may decide that a spelling bee will not work, you know. They may need to write the words out as practice before the actual test."

"Uh-huh." Gail's right hand begins to shake. She rests her elbow on the table and places her quivering hand on her forehead. When Cheryl's face becomes a blur and the tape recorder all but disappears, she holds her head down. Her wool skirt soaks up the dampness like a sponge.

Gail appreciates the fact that Cheryl does not stop. She knows if she talks much more, the flood gates will really open. As Cheryl continues, Gail struggles to regain composure. She feels a tinge of pain as she bites her bottom lip. Both hands resting on her lap tug at the tissue.

"But we'll talk about those sorts of things later. Okay. Tell me about the other side of your teaching experience, though. We've talked about the kids. What about your colleagues and you?"

"Oh. They've been very nice. Very supportive." Gail tries to stop the quiver in her voice. Cheryl's face is clear to her now. She detects a look of pity in Cheryl's eyes. Her mind goes back to her sister's words: "We Simmons can accept any challenge; we are winners!"

"Great! I'm glad to hear that. Are you learning the ropes?"

Gail avoids looking directly at Cheryl. "I think so. Wilma Berry has been fantastic. I feel like I can go to her and ask her some things. Whether it's about. . . What is tray duty?" Do they need a note for tray duty?" Gail laughs. "Or . . . up to, you know, something silly. Any little thing or big thing. And things I just run across, I'll ask her … funny little questions that I have not thought about in years." Gail hands the box of tissues back to Cheryl.

"Right. OK. Would you say Wilma Berry has taken you under her wings? Or has anyone?" Cheryl swings her chair around and places the box of tissues back on her desk.

"Well, she's always there when I need her. She doesn't come in my room. I don't think she seeks me out."

"I see." Gail jumps when she hears the sudden click of the tape recorder. As Cheryl's long, well-manicured fingers reach toward the eject button, Gail places her hands back on her lap so they will not be visible. She wonders how Cheryl can dress so neatly every day. She always dresses in a business suit and every strand of her short, dark brown hair seems to always be in place. Her shoes always match her outfit perfectly.

"But, I don't bother her when I don't need her. I mean ….imposing."

"Wonderful! That's great. But no one has actually taken you under their wings? No one has said, 'Hey let me show you this, or I'm going to take care of you?"

"Well . . . actually, Lucy Cummins has, although she's new, too. She's helped me quite a bit because there were some things that . . . being new, totally new, is different from being just new to this school."

"Right. Right." Cheryl agrees.

There is a long pause which makes Gail feel uncomfortable, so she continues. "Like with some of the things with textbooks. There are procedures. And then she's helped me with some of the machines. She was telling me about some of them that I wasn't real sure about."

"Right."

"Some different things . . . ah . . . stuff that's going to be the same from one school to another."

"Yeah. So she's using her previous experience. And you don't have that to fall back on," Cheryl adds.

"And we both have a common bond because we're both new to the school. But, yet, she's got this other stuff that she knows about and she shares it with me."

"Right. That's wonderful!" Cheryl seems pleased that Gail's colleagues are reaching out to her. Gail decides to say more on the topic of her colleagues. It's certainly more pleasant than talking about her classes. Cheryl's smile is reassuring.

"And she really helps. She has come over a couple of times and said this or that and asked me if I knew about a certain requirement," Gail adds.

"That's great! I didn't realize that was going on. So, you think maybe she realizes what you're going through?"

"Uh-huh."

"She remembers the way it was when she first started?"

"I think so."

"That's interesting. And both of you are new." Cheryl is obviously pleased with this information. She smiles broadly, revealing the small gap in her teeth on the left side. Cheryl's smile is very inviting, but Gail remembers that some of her colleagues have told her that Cheryl's smile is deceiving. The teacher across the hall tells Gail that she will smile one moment and hand you a written reprimand the next. But Gail feels she and Cheryl have established a rapport. She trusts Cheryl and hasn't seen any signs of deception at all. But, still, her sister has warned her to be cautious.

"And we're both new. We both went to the same university, you know. And we are about the same age."

"I didn't know that."

"Yeah. We have a few things in common. Same age. Same school." Gail feels really relaxed now.

"That's great! Is anyone telling you any secrets?"

"What secrets?"

"About the school?"

"No. . . ."

"Are you picking up any cues from the principals or colleagues?"

"A little bit, maybe. Maybe some from the principals. I worry somewhat about sending people to the office or discussing the students with the principals." The back of Gail's neck feels warm. She places her hand there momentarily, hoping to stop the burning sensation.

"Really?" Cheryl asks.

"Like... I talked to Mr. Clinard about my Career Education class." Gail pauses for a long time. In her lap her trembling hands play a tug of war with the moist piece of rumpled tissue. She tears the tissue as she continues. "Because I was having such a hard time with some of the seniors and because that class is so large."

Cheryl hands Gail the box of tissues. "Right."

"And he ah . . . I worry about that because I didn't know whether to tough it out and not mention it, you know."

"Right. So, did you pick up any cues from him?"

Gail finds it difficult to continue. "It was just that . . . ah. . . I was worried."

"You were worried about the ramifications?"

"Yeah. I was worried, but I think he seemed a little worried afterwards."

"Afterwards?" Cheryl asks for clarification.

"But I felt better after our conference about the observation. So, I hope that ..."

"Yeah. I see what you mean. You feel that maybe he saw a very bleak picture during his observation, and that things are improving now? And that he may not know?"

"Yeah. He thinks that things are still up in the air and he has lots of things on his mind and he may just think about it. He just goes on and sees that bleak picture." Gail's eyelids feel sore as she continues to rub them.

"Yes. OK. So, you may want to touch base with him again and let him know that things are better now," Cheryl suggests. Her voice is low and sympathetic.

"Um-hum. I will." Gail rubs her hands against her skirt again. She struggles to keep them from shaking.

Cheryl watches Gail's face carefully. "You said you felt better after your conference with Mr. Clinard. Why?"

"Well . . . after he visited my class," Gail explains, "I received this sealed envelope from him instructing me to meet with him after school. I just knew he was going to be very critical, but he realizes I don't have the best students in that class. He wasn't angry with me, but very supportive. I just hope he knows that things are better now. He seems to really be concerned." She looks at Cheryl for reassurance.

"Yes, he is concerned. He really wants to help you through this. All of us do. He's supposed to be meeting with me about that class, too. We probably need to separate some of those characters, but it is so hard to reschedule students at this late date," Cheryl adds.

Gail feels a tinge of guilt. She wonders how many of the other new teachers are requiring so much of the principals' time.

"So, how do you feel about teaching at this point?" Cheryl asks.

Gail pauses for a long time. As she looks down, she notices that a thread of the gold carpet has been broken and is beginning to unravel. "I'm equally satisfied and dissatisfied, I guess. There are just really satisfying things and then there are some real frustrating things."

"OK. We need to elaborate on those. What are the things that seem to frustrate you?" Cheryl asks.

"Oh, I think it's the discipline. When I get right down to it and really think about what that one thing is, it's the discipline."

"OK. Classroom management and discipline."

"Um-hum. Um-hum."

"OK. Can you think of any changes that would increase your level of satisfaction here? We've mentioned improving discipline and classroom management skills. What else?"

"Oh. I think I'm fairly well organized. But, you have to be super organized to teach."

"Yes. Yes. Definitely."

"Super organized. So that is something I still need to do. Set up things at home. There's this big table that's awfully full."

"Yes. I understand. What are the things you like least about teaching?"

"Right now what I like least about it is I have very little personal time. Very little."

"OK."

"But I expect that to get better. It's taking just about all my time to do it. Day and night." Gail lets out a deep sigh. "All weekend. And that's not good. You can't do that forever." Gail glances at the large clock on the wall facing her.

"No. No, you can't." Cheryl agrees. "But you certainly feel that this is a temporary situation? Because you're so new and you're having to deal from the bottom up with nothing to draw from in terms of resources; like an old lesson plan that you know works? You don't have anything at your fingertips."

"Nothing at all."

"If I ask you what you lose by being a teacher rather than working in another occupation, what would you say?"

"What would I lose?"

"Yes. What are you losing? What do you lose by being a teacher rather than being in sales or in something else?"

"It's just right now I lose time for myself."

"OK."

"And that's important to me," Gail reiterates. Gail is surprised at this revelation. She sees that the interviews with Cheryl help her to stay in touch with her feelings. Up until now, she has not really known how important her personal time is. Now she sees how much she misses time to just shop or watch a good movie on television. It's hard to remember the last time she and her close friend, Jeff, went out to dinner. Lately when he has called she has had too much work to do. She has not heard from Jeff in weeks.

"So, you did have more time for yourself when you were in sales than you do now?"

"Yes. Well, sales is a lonely job. Most of that driving kind of tires you out. But, it's the free time for myself that I enjoyed. Just regular old free time."

"So, you miss that part of it?"

"Yes, I do. Well, I don't think people go into teaching for the money because there's more money elsewhere for most people."

"Then, what do you like most about teaching?"

There is a pause. "Well . . . that goes back to my original desire to help people. I've always wanted to help people."

"Sure. Sure. And that's rewarding for you?"

"Yes. What's most rewarding are the times that I know I have helped a student or a group of students and they have learned."

"OK. Alright. Can you think of anything else that could have made the four weeks that you've been employed here better for you?"

"Ummmm . . ."

"We've talked about having had more time for preparation and planning," Cheryl reminds her.

"Having one preparation would have helped. Or two," Cheryl adds.

"That's certainly legitimate," Gail agrees.

"Yes. One thing that makes it so difficult for you is that you're preparing for so many different subjects. The AP English, English 1, Eleventh Grade Fundamentals, and Career Education. That's four preparations, wouldn't you say?"

"I know. We've talked about it. There's a little bit of the same thing that I can do with the ninth grade and the eleventh grade. The ninth graders are wild, though."

Gail knows what Cheryl is going to say next. "You remember we talked earlier about taking the ninth grade honors group rather than the AP?" Cheryl asks.

"I remember. Probably it was a week after we had talked about this that I said to myself when she offers it to me again, I'm going to take it. Definitely."

"Yeah." Gail senses a bit of irritation in Cheryl's tone. She wonders if she angered Cheryl by refusing her offer. She wonders if her sister gave her the right advice.

"But, I think now I feel a little better about it. I talked to some people. I ran down some other AP teachers. I went to talk to the teacher at the magnet school. He's great! I also went and talked to a friend in Jeffersonville."

"That's wonderful!" So, you're reaching out for resources." Cheryl seems genuinely pleased as she smiles.

"That's great! How do you feel at this point in terms of being here? Do you feel more like an outsider or an insider?"

"I guess I feel like an insider. This is so much more of a stable working situation than I've had in a while. And I come to the same place and see the same people often."

"That's not bad for four weeks, you know. That's not bad at all," Cheryl reiterates.

It's obvious that Gail's mind is on something else. She doesn't look at Cheryl, but out into space. "I hope, as I said before, that Mr. Clinard is not still concerned." She looks at the clock on the wall and reaches for her purse. She sighs as she realizes that it is time to face her next class.

Thought Questions

Chapter 6 – Rainy Days

1. What steps has Gail taken to improve her situation?

2. Do you feel that Gail will be successful? Why? Why not?

3. Gail seems to really be concerned about Mr. Clinard's impression of her teaching abilities. If you were Gail, how would you handle this situation?

4. In this chapter, Gail states, "… and I can't really determine what way it's going to go." What does this statement tell you about Gail?

5. Cheryl asks Gail how she feels about teaching. What do you think the statement below symbolizes?

Gail pauses for a long time. As she looks down, she notices that a thread of the gold carpet has been broken and is beginning to unravel.

Chapter 7

THE FIRST SNOW

Another sealed envelope is delivered to the fifth period. Gail lays it on her desk and waits for her students to report to their next class. If the envelope contains bad news, she wants to be alone when she reads it. A short time later, she reads the typed reminder from Mr. Clinard that she is to report to a conference with him and Cheryl so they can agree upon some definitive steps for her to take in dealing with discipline problems in her classes.

Gail detects a certain chill in the air when she reports to Cheryl's office at the end of the school day. Though Gail has learned to feel very comfortable reporting to Cheryl's office, Mr. Clinard's presence seems to add an aura of formality and discomfort. It even seems strange that the tape recorder is missing from the table.

Cheryl sits at the head of the conference table, while Mr. Clinard sits by the window. Gail decides to occupy one of the chairs closest to the front door.

Mr. Clinard, his bulging stomach visible even when he is seated, wipes his brow and begins. "Mrs. Rossman, I apologize for scheduling this meeting after school, but it was the best I could do. I tell ya, it is almost impossible to get away from the office during the school day. So I hope you and Miss Simmons don't mind."

"Not at all, Mr. Clinard," Cheryl says. "The scheduling is perfect. How was your day, Miss Simmons?"

"Today wasn't so bad," Gail says, rather hesitantly. Gail's words are barely audible above the loud, desperate voices that shout messages over the intercom as the school day ends and various extra-curricular activities begin.

"Well, the last twelve weeks or so have been very difficult for you," Mr. Clinard states. "So I thought, with Mrs. Rossman's help, we could begin to turn things around." He begins to squint again, as if the sun is bothering him. "Exactly what is it we can do to help you, Miss Simmons?" he asks.

"Well. . . I don't really know. All I know is that my students are not behaving the way I expected them to." Her voice is barely audible as she continues. "Sometimes I wonder, ah . . . well, it seems like. . . I remember my school. When I was in school, we had a little more respect for people, but maybe it's just the times."

"Oh, that's probably true. I think there was a lot of fear of teachers then," Cheryl says.

"Some of our students still have that, but most of them don't," Mr. Clinard adds.

"They don't!" Gail's voice is louder now.

"Not only that, they relate to their parents differently, too," Mr. Clinard says. His hands are folded across his stomach. He twirls one thumb around the other. There is an uncomfortable silence.

"Do they?" Gail looks at Cheryl for confirmation.

"Yeah. They're given much more flexibility at home than we were. And that makes a difference in how they respond to authority figures." Cheryl explains.

"One of the things we can try to do that may help, Gail, is to reduce the size of that career education class. I will give you some forms so that students in that class can write down their current schedules. We will take it from there." Cheryl goes out and brings a stack of blue forms to Gail. Her stockings, plum pumps, and plum suit match perfectly. "Hopefully, we can find another class for some of them," Cheryl adds, as Gail grabs the forms.

"Two students were taken out last six weeks, but I received three new students a couple of days later," Gail explains.

Mr. Clinard interrupts, "Now, I understand that the fifth period is not the only class you're having difficulty with. Am I right?"

"Well, I am having a little trouble getting the A.P. students to do their reading and turn in their work on time, but they're not discipline problems at all." She wonders what Cheryl is writing on the pad in front of her.

"So what about your other classes, Gail?" Cheryl asks. She puts her pen down and waits.

Gail looks at the clock and thinks how wonderful it would be if she were home. She wonders how any of this is going to help. "They get a little noisy at times," Gail confesses. "But the fifth period is my worst."

"We're going to try and do something about that,' Mr. Clinard states. "But there are a few things you need to do. One of those is to raise your voice and develop a mean look. You are simply too nice to them." He looks at Gail, still twirling his thumbs.

"I think he's right, Gail," Cheryl says. "But, you may also want to attend a discipline workshop at the Teacher Center. Here's the schedule. This may be very helpful. In the meantime, Mr. Clinard and I will make a concerted effort to visit your classes more often. OK?"

"Yes, that's fine," Gail says.

"Is there anything else we need to talk about, Miss Simmons?" Mr. Clinard asks. He looks at his watch and rises.

"No," Gail whispers.

"You just let us know, now, if you need us. Things will get better if we work at it. We'll see you tomorrow."

Gail makes a quick exit, being closest to the door. Out of the corner of her eye, she seems to see Mr. Clinard shake his head. The concerned look on Cheryl's face is matched by the dark clouds rising over the horizon as Gail rushes toward her car.

All of these efforts, however, do not seem to be enough to turn the situation around. Gail's level of frustration seems to be high at her next interview with Cheryl.

"Ok, Gail, the last time we met was October 16. So, that's been a good long while. Four weeks."

"An entire month," Gail confirms.

"How do you rate the last four weeks from one to ten?"

"It seems like about two years," Gail laughs.

"Does it?"

'It does. It really does. It is hard to put a number on it. I don't. . . Sometimes it's a ten and then sometimes it's a one. Sometimes it's a six or whatever. So I guess I'll go in the middle. About a five."

"Five? Okay. Sounds reasonable. How did you come up with that rating? On what basis?" Cheryl asks.

"Well. . . Just that. . . ." She pauses and twists a lock of her dark hair around her forefinger. "There's some high days and some low days."

"What are your major concerns right now?"

"Well, I still have problems with discipline. Some of it is better because I think I've got a better relationship in some of the classes. Even though it may be a better sort of rowdy relationship." Gail laughs nervously. "It's a little louder than I'd like it to be. I think I've got a good rapport with the classes, except maybe the fifth period."

"Fifth period is better, but not what I'd like it to be. I'm gonna lose the fifth period though in another four weeks. It's only the class, I think. . . ." Her chin begins to quiver. "I'm really glad, to be honest. It will be time to say good-bye to some of them."

"Yeah. Next semester you'll have a chance to start over. When I was trying to get some of them rescheduled, though, I noticed that they were scheduled to be back with you the second semester."

"I do have maybe four or five from this group who will be back with me again." Gail sighs deeply. "I'm going to have a real serious talk with them. And if I have any real serious problems with them, "I'll just send them out."

"What about mean looks? Have you worked on those?"

"I don't know. I think so. Sometimes that works and sometimes it doesn't. Maybe it's gotten better, but it's not perfect."

Gail wonders if Cheryl's new line of questioning has anything to do with her research project. She can see that Cheryl is really trying to help. "I've tried with mean looks. I think it's the same as the voice. It's hard for me to have a mean look. I believe I'm just not very good with those mean looks."

"Well, if you're going to teach, you're going to have to develop one," Cheryl says emphatically.

"Um-hum. That's what my sister tells me, too. We were talking about that a few days ago."

Cheryl's large eyes grow even larger as she continues. "You can't survive otherwise. And of course, the good thing about it is that once the kids get to know that look, then they'll behave accordingly and you won't have to use it every day."

"Um-hum."

"Learn to use your eyes very effectively and dramatically so that you can make a point without having to stop in the middle of an activity to correct a student. You can flash your eyes on the student and he knows what you mean." Cheryl flashes her large eyes from one corner to the next.

Gail does not remember seeing her look so mean. Her jaw is taut and her nostrils flared.

"I see," Gail says. She is a bit amused to see another side of Cheryl, who is usually very poised and unruffled by whatever is going on. She wonders how you learn to change your voice and facial expressions that way. Gail thinks maybe she should have taken some acting classes, instead of so many classes in educational theory.

"OK? You have to be animated when you try to let the students know you mean business." Cheryl gives Gail several examples of animated responses.

"Oh . . . that's interesting," Gail confesses.

"Well, all of this is kind of on the side as far as teaching is concerned. It's stuff you have to pick up. And you have to develop your own way of making students know that you are serious and that you mean business."

"Right."

"You have to figure out a way to be convincing," Cheryl emphasizes. "But you said things had improved for you. Have they?" Cheryl asks, as she glances at her interview guide.

"I think so."

"How do you know? What makes you think that things have improved?"

"Maybe it's because . . . I hope this isn't it, but maybe it's because they're not bothering me as much. But, I think that they'll get quieter quicker when I ask them to."

"OK. Have you changed the manner in which you do that?"

"Well . . . maybe I have. Maybe I've gotten a little louder or firmer." Gail feels that Cheryl is not pleased with her answers. Suddenly, the cushioned chair feels hard.

"Or, if you've been doing it much more readily, that will make a difference. See, another part of the discipline process is that you have to be on your toes. In other words, you don't let them begin the talking in the first place. OK?"

"Um-hum. Of course, that's a problem. When it starts at the first of the year, you are new and you don't know what patterns to look for. And before you know it, the patterns have already developed. It's no going back, you know." Gail is proud of the answer she gives for this one.

"One of the things teachers have to learn to do that goes with the territory, though, is to repeat themselves. Whatever you do, you have to be consistent with it or it won't work." Cheryl has the concerned look on her face again.

"When they don't have paper and pencil, it just drives me nuts!" Gail says, gritting her teeth.

"Don't let it drive you nuts. Figure out a way to deal with it. That's one of the joys of teaching." Cheryl smiles and flips the tape to the other side.

"But, I just don't have it. I'm not an endless supply of pencils. I didn't even have a pencil sharpener in my room until the other day. Now that the custodian has finally installed a pencil sharpener, someone wants to use it every five minutes. Sometimes I think we were better off without it." She lets out a deep sigh and tugs at a loose thread on her black skirt.

"Just stay on them and they'll begin to realize that in Miss Simmons' class you've got to bring paper and pencil. Being consistent makes the difference. You've got to keep reminding them that they must bring paper and pencil to class."

"OK," Gail states.

"If you mention whatever it is that is important to you every day, it will finally soak in. But it takes mentioning every day. If it's being late, it takes mentioning every day. If it's coming without paper and pencil, it takes mentioning every day. Whatever it is, you've got to mention it to them every day." Cheryl gestures for emphasis. Gail notices that Cheryl's feet barely touch the floor as she swings her chair from side to side. She wonders how such a short lady can wield so much power. She has seen how the students respond to Cheryl and knows that the teachers respect her. Even Dr. Reed seems to respect her wishes for the most part.

"Um-hum," Gail says, listening closely.

"You see, that's just part of it . . . part of the job. But I enjoy it. I love it!" Cheryl smiles broadly.

"You know . . . well . . . I'm still thinking about it. I don't know if I love it or not. There are times when I do. And times when I am just ready to say forget it. I've just had too many that have really gotten under my skin."

"But . . . that's typical. That's normal. I would think once a month every teacher has that feeling," Cheryl assures her.

"Sometimes I wonder . . . God, is it worth it?"

"I would think, once a month, even our best teachers feel that way because teaching is so draining. It can take so much out of you if you're giving the way you should as a teacher. You are going to be exhausted on some days and you're going to have some terribly frustrating days because you are dealing with groups of people who haven't reached a certain level of maturity."

"Uh-hum. And you spend all this time preparing things for them." Gail sighs as she looks at the familiar clock.

"Exactly." Cheryl shakes her head in agreement.

"And then it's kind of hit or miss some days. It's like maybe you got some of it across and some you didn't. It's just . . . I worked all of that time, you know," Gail says. The deep long sighs continue. Her neck begins to feel hot again. She pulls a tissue from the box that Cheryl hands her and wipes her eyes. "It seems like such a waste of time."

"Don't be so hard on yourself," Cheryl assures her. "The first year is supposed to be the building year, the learning year, you know."

"OK."

"You know, you had a set of expectations when you first came aboard as to what teaching would be like. How are things different from what you expected?"

"Ah . . . I guess I thought I would feel that I had gotten through a bit more than I think I have."

"OK."

"That I would just be here. I would be teaching and they would just learn it, and. . . ."

"All right. I see what you're saying. The traditional picture of the teacher at the blackboard explaining everything and the kids are bright eyed and interested and taking it in. The picture that you see in the textbooks. Is that what you expected?"

"Right. Right. But they are not like that!" Gail says forcefully. Once again, she looks down at the frayed piece of thread sticking up in the gold carpet.

"No."

"I thought maybe there would be some problems with discipline, but I just didn't think it through."

"Probably not. You don't picture those things, generally."

"No! No! And I was really excited about this job, too. But you don't picture problems when you are excited about something."

"Do you feel the picture you created came from what your sister had shared with you or from when you were in school? Where did those pictures you created come from?" Cheryl asks.

"Probably more from when I was in school." Gail's mind goes back to her childhood school days. It seemed so easy for her teachers back then. All she remembers is that they sat at their desks and gave everyone orders. She doesn't remember anyone challenging them. She doesn't remember noisy classrooms or disrespectful remarks. All she remembers is that the teachers taught and the students learned.

Gail continues, "My sister makes it seem very easy, though."

"So maybe I thought that because she had it so easy, it would be easy for me. But it's not that easy. She kind of reinforced it. She lied." The tears increase as Gail fumbles for another tissue. She finds this whole situation somewhat amusing. She doesn't know if she should laugh or cry. She smiles in spite of the tears.

"She probably forgot. She's been teaching for some time. She painted a good picture for you and it didn't work out." Cheryl laughs.

"This week, I've been sleeping a lot. I don't know how I've had the time to do anything else. I've gone home, I've tried to do work for the next day and I've gone right to bed. And I've been getting too much sleep. I suspect that I must be depressed about something."

"Yeah?"

"Yeah. It is usually when I'm depressed that I sleep a lot."

"Right. So . . . how do . . .?"

Gail interrupts, "How could I not have known when I grew up in a family of teachers? Why didn't anyone tell me about the constant noise, the endless papers to grade, and the hours of reading and preparation required just to keep a page or two ahead of the students? Why? Why? Why?" Gail feels her whole body begin to shake.

"Gail, you're being much too hard on yourself." Gail feels the warmth when Cheryl's hand envelopes her own.

"No, I'm not, Cheryl. I really think maybe I need to do something else."

"Look, Gail. You will feel better on Monday. Take this weekend to get plenty of rest and sort things through. I think you're just exhausted." Gail deliberately avoids Cheryl's gaze. She wonders why Cheryl doesn't make it easy on her. Gail thinks to herself, "Why doesn't Mr. Clinard and Cheryl just tell me the truth? Why don't they just tell me that I'll never make it as a teacher?"

Gail grabs for her purse and the stack of papers she must grade over the weekend. Cheryl hands them both to her as Gail rushes toward the door.

As she steps out into the cold, wintry air she breathes deeply. The cold air stings as it dries the dampness from her cheeks. She walks fast so that she can get to her car before anyone else sees her. As her car turns the corner and Melrose is no longer in view, the rain begins to fall. Within moments, the rain has turned to snow.

Thought Questions

Chapter 7 – The First Snow

1. How do you feel about Mr. Clinard's advice for Gail to raise her voice and develop a mean look?

2. Cheryl tells Gail to attend the discipline workshop at the Teacher Center. How do you feel about Cheryl's advice?

3. Cheryl later tells Gail that if she is going to survive as a teacher, she must develop a mean look and learn to elevate her voice. Do you agree with Cheryl? Why? Why not?

4. Cheryl also tells Gail that she has to develop her own way of making students know that she is serious and that she means business. Do you agree or disagree? Why? Why not?

5. What other advice does Cheryl give Gail? How appropriate do you feel this advice is for Gail?

6. How do you explain Gail's exasperation at being from a family of successful teachers and not feeling that she can be a successful teacher?

Chapter 8

RIDING OUT THE STORM

Gail Simmons sleeps in a tiny bunk bed with a gleaming brass frame. A brass trunk rests at the foot and a vanity table sets beneath the window. Outside the window, a crab apple tree bereft of its leaves groans beneath the weight of the snow on its branches. The snow storm has ended as suddenly as it began and most of the streets are passable. School bus drivers have been directed to run only the snow routes.

She wakes up with a start. She has forgotten something. She has forgotten to grade the A.P. students' term papers. "How could I be so stupid?" she thinks. This is the last week of the semester and all grades must be submitted by Friday. She has already heard what happens to teachers who do not get their grades in on time. She grimaces at the thought of suffering the humiliation of having her name announced over the intercom.

Still in her morning robe, she tackles the stack of unfinished term papers waiting patiently at the kitchen table. She remembers how she fell asleep while trying to sort out the last paragraph of one of the more poorly written papers. She wonders how some of the students ever qualified for an advanced placement course.

Gail finishes the last paper at 5:40 a.m. and turns on the shower one hour later than usual. If she rushes, she feels she can still make it on time. Just as she steps out of the shower, her phone rings.

"Gail, it's me, Jeff." The deep voice on the other end sounds desperate. "You've asked me not to bother you, but I miss you. You say you're busy, and I've tried to understand. But I can't believe you're so busy we can't make it to a movie once a month. If you're spending your time with someone else, Gail, just tell me. And I promise I will leave you alone."

After an awkward pause, Gail tells Jeff what she realizes he does not want to hear. "Jeff, I am so sorry. I realize this has been difficult for you. I know it's been three months since we have gone out, but I've just had a hard time keeping my head above water. Maybe during the Christmas holidays. Ok? Look, I've got to go or I'll be late!"

Gail hangs up the phone and tries to thrust Jeff out of her mind as she searches her closet for something to wear. "Sure, I'd like to go to a movie. But if I go to a movie, I don't survive. The Simmons are survivors! Right? Right." She has been holding these conversations with herself much more often lately. They help her to maintain her sanity and a much needed sense of humor.

"If I allow myself to dwell on Jeff I will lose my perspective," she whispers to herself as she buttons her white blouse. "But I'm being so unfair to him. My sister has a family and she manages. Why can't I?" Gail picks up the phone and dials Jeff's number.

"Hello. Hello. Who is this?" The voice on the other end sounds angry.

"I can't do it," she says as she places the phone back on the hook. "I spend every waking moment preparing for these classes, so I know what will happen if I take one night off. I can't do it! I just can't do it! Jeff will just have to wait. It's a good thing I kept my phone off the hook all weekend. My sister told me it was the only way I would get all my work done."

"Oh, God! Why am I doing this?" she asks. "My keys." She looks on her dresser and around her brass bed. "Where have I put those keys? I've got to get out of here!" She slips on her navy blue coat and searches each pocket frantically. No keys. She walks through every room in her small apartment. No Keys. She grabs her students' term papers from the kitchen table and shoves them in her leather attaché.

"I'll just have to catch a ride with someone," she says as she thrusts open the front door. The cold air stings her cheeks and numbs her ankles. It's much colder than she imagined. She yearns to go back inside. But the metallic sound she hears as soon as the door closes makes her smile and stops her heart from racing.

"You dummy!" she says. "How could you have left the keys in the door? You've got to get a hold of yourself!"

The long drive to Melrose gives Gail a chance to clear her head and plan her lesson for A.P. English, her first class of the day. The bell sounds just as she parks. Dr. Reed is thumbing through the stack of morning announcements when she enters the lobby. Gail doesn't want him to see her sign in late, so she proceeds to her room. Several students are scurrying past her rushing to their classes.

Gail's students are standing in the hall waiting for her to open up her room. She is embarrassed, but she tells herself at least they'll be happy to receive their term papers.

Not long after her students are settled she hears her name called. "Miss Simmons? Miss Simmons?" She recognizes the voice as that of Mrs. Jones, the receptionist.

"Yes." There is silence.

"I was just checking to see if you were here. You didn't sign in."

The students snicker. "I'll be right down," Gail says.

"That's OK. I'll sign you in myself. I just need to know that your class is covered. You have a nice day. I'll take care of everything."

Gail smiles to herself and wonders what she would do without Mrs. Jones. She has always been exceptionally nice to her. Mrs. Jones always comes through for her when she's in a pinch. That's more than she can say for some of her colleagues, whom she has learned to avoid.

Lately she feels that they talk about her behind her back. She notices that when she enters the faculty lounge, conversations seem to stop. She no longer confides in Wilma Berry or Mrs. Easley. She doesn't trust anyone. She's afraid if she asks for help, she will be perceived as a failure. At least if she keeps everything to herself, they will never know how bad things are. She feels secure in the knowledge that no one really knows what goes on in her classroom but herself and her students.

It's pretty obvious that no one can help her anyway. Mr. Clinard and Mrs. Rossman promised to help her, and what did that accomplish? Nothing. It was their frequent visits that signaled to all of her colleagues that she was in trouble. The students even asked her if the principals felt that she couldn't do her job.

For Gail, this whole situation has been humiliating. She feels that the negatives have outweighed the positives. She wants so much to be a successful teacher. But at what price? Must she give up all of her personal time? Her social life? Her dignity?

Despite all of her apprehensions, the rest of the day goes well for Gail. She gives out papers in all of her classes, an event her students obviously await with eagerness. Somehow, when Gail returns her students' papers, there is less complaining when she makes new assignments. The only dissatisfied student she encounters is a young lady in A.P. who feels the grade on her term paper is unfair. Gail feels it was certainly worth the effort to spend her whole weekend grading those papers. Her students show their appreciation by working quietly for her all day.

Even so, Gail feels depressed as she leaves the parking lot at the end of the day. She discovers that a relatively quiet classroom gives her too much time to think. Half way home she finds herself taking an alternative route and heading toward her sister's house. She is relieved when she can pull into the driveway, out of the flow of heavy traffic. Her eyes have been clouding up all the way, making it difficult for her to see the approaching vehicles.

Rosie comes out to meet her. By now she knows the sound of Gail's car engine. "Gail," she says. "I'm glad to see you. I've been worried about you." They embrace briefly. "You're as skinny as a rail. C'mon, let's get something to eat. I've just put on a pot of fresh, homemade vegetable soup."

"I'm not hungry, Sis," Gail says, her voice cracking. The house feels toasty warm and inviting. The wonderful aroma coming from the kitchen takes Gail back to her childhood. The sweet smell of okra, corn, tomatoes, diced potatoes and peppers increases her appetite. She sits at the kitchen table in the chair that has been her favorite for years, the one right across from the picture window that allows her to look over the entire neighborhood or get lost in her dreams.

Rosie places a coffee mug in front of her, filled with piping hot coffee and cream. "Now, what is this about not being hungry?" Rosie tilts Gail's chin upward so she can look into her eyes.

"Are you depressed again?" she asks as she fills a cup for herself. She sits directly across from Gail, not concerned about the outside view.

"You know, Sis," Gail begins, putting her cup down very gingerly, "I've been giving this job a lot of thought." She looks deeply within her sister's eyes. "In fact, it's all I've been thinking about lately." She takes a deep breath and reaches for her cup. "Actually, it's all I've had time to think about," Gail manages a small laugh.

Rosie is unusually quiet. "In fact," Gail continues, "It's the time that bothers me the most. I spend all of this time preparing for these classes and within five or ten minutes the whole, wonderfully perfect lesson is destroyed." Her eyes begin to water.

"You mean that happens to you, too? I thought I was the only teacher who had ever had a lesson demolished," says Rosie, and both laugh. While Gail laughs, a single teardrop rolls down her cheek and rests at the bottom of her chin. She rubs her chin with the back of her hand and shakes her head in disbelief.

"I can't believe this is happening to me." She shakes her head, sighing. "It looks like I've jumped out of the frying pan into the fire. For once in my life I wanted to be like my big sister and make my parents proud. I wanted to teach." She looks out the window, longingly. "I wanted to follow in my parents' footsteps, to leave my mark on society. Sounds quite noble, doesn't it, Sis?" She asks, rather facetiously.

"Teaching is a noble profession, Gail. But you don't become expert at it overnight. It takes time and patience with yourself. You are extremely patient with other folk, but not with Gail. You and I both know that. Now, am I right?" She pushes Gail to respond.

Gail puckers her lips the way she used to when they were younger, especially when she knew that her sister had won another argument. "Yep, you are right. So, what am I supposed to do? Ride out the storm?"

"What would a Simmons do?

"Ride out the storm!" they both say in unison. The laughter comes natural and feels good to Gail as they raise their mugs in a toast.

Thought Questions

Chapter 8 – Riding Out the Storm

1. How would you describe the relationship between Gail and Rosie?

2. Why does Gail feel that she should alienate herself from her colleagues?

3. Who in the organization does Gail still trust? Provide justification for your answer.

4. It appears that time has become a major concern of Gail's. Can you think of some ways Gail can carve out more time for herself?

5. What are the implications of Gail's reaction to Jeff? How would you handle this situation?

Chapter 9

AGAINST THE WIND

The storm seems to dissipate by the time Gail helps herself to a brimming cup of Rosie's warm vegetable soup and sleeps for twelve wonderfully quiet, undisturbed hours. A visit and long talk with Rosie is always therapeutic. She takes her phone off the hook again and allows the restful sleep to heal her physically and emotionally drained body. She welcomes Tuesday morning at Melrose with renewed confidence and determination.

She signs in, checks her mailbox and occupies a seat in the reception area to peruse the tidbits of information her mailbox contains. Other faculty members scurry in and out, signing names and emptying mailboxes. Their greetings vary from cheerful, to solemn, to a mere mumble. Some enter and leave in complete silence, engrossed in their own thoughts; lost in their own world. The groups of students milling around in the lobby grow larger as the time for the first bell of the morning draws near. A disgruntled parent comes in and asks to see the principal.

"Good morning, Gail. I haven't seen you in a good little while," a cheerful voice states. Gail looks up to see Lucy Cummings, the friend she knew in college who now teaches around the corner from her.

"Hello, Lucy. How are you?" Gail puts her papers aside and rises from her chair.

"If I can just get all of this paperwork done for the semester, I will be fine. It takes so much energy! I don't know where the energy would come from if I didn't get to run every day!" Her warm, inviting smile seems to consume her entire face. She has such small features and a wispy frame. Gail now understands why she is so small. Not a day goes by that Gail does not see her running around the track in back of the school.

Lucy opens the door and they move out into the lobby to head toward their rooms. "I've made out the exam for each of my classes, so I feel pretty caught up," Gail says, wondering what else remains to be done.

At the ringing of the morning bell they are momentarily separated by a throng of exuberant students. Lucy, short and petite, is hidden from Gail's view until the throng passes. "You have made out a yellow course card for each of your students, haven't you?" Lucy asks as she catches back up with Gail.

"No one told me to."

"Well, it will keep you from having to rush on the day after exams." They climb the steps to the second floor. Gail normally uses the elevator, but Lucy has boundless energy. "We have two exams today, right?" Lucy confirms.

Lucy continues before Gail answers, "On Wednesday, Gail, you will be expected to put these yellow course grade cards for each of your students in their homeroom teachers' mailboxes. They have to be filled out with their grades for the first three six weeks, their exam grade, and their semester average. You didn't know?" Lucy looks at Gail with compassion as she unlocks her room.

"Mrs. Rossman told me about the cards, but I thought I could do those over the Christmas holidays." Gail feels a burning sensation in the pit of her stomach.

"Oh, no! All of this has to be done by Friday morning. Friday is the day all grades have to be recorded on the students' permanent records."

Lucy is at her desk now. "Mrs. Rossman explained all this at the faculty meeting yesterday afternoon. Remember? Anyway, you need to get an early start so you won't get behind. Believe me, it is no fun when everyone is waiting for your cards." She opens her desk drawer and pulls out a set of yellow cards held together by a single rubber band.

"This is my set for the first period, Gail. Feel free to look at these. Here. Why don't you take this one to use as an example? You can give it back to me later."

"I don't even have any of these cards, Lucy. Where did you get these?"

"I'll go to Mrs. Easley's room and get them for you. I have to talk to her about another matter, anyway," Lucy says.

"I really appreciate this, Lucy. What would I do without your friendship?"

"What are friends for, huh?" Lucy disappears among throngs of students lingering in the hall waiting for the tardy bell to sound before they move toward their classrooms.

Gail scurries down to her room and unlocks the door for eight of her sixteen students enrolled in A.P. Just as she puts her things on her desk she hears the announcement:

"Miss Simmons, come to the office, please.

Miss Simmons, I need to see you in my office."

Gail's heart skips. The authoritative, urgent voice is that of Dr. Reed. She feels stunned and confused. "What am I to do with my class?" she wonders as she writes out an assignment to help them review for their exam.

Lucy appears with the yellow course cards just as she is about to dart out the door. "Dr. Reed has called me to the office. What am I to do with my students?"

"How many do you have?" Lucy asks.

"About sixteen. But they're good kids," she adds.

"Oh." Lucy's eyes brighten. "This is the A.P. class I've heard so much about."

"What do you mean?" Gail asks. "What have you heard? I want to know."

"Miss Simmons, come to the main office!

I need to see you in my office. Miss Simmons!"

"Look, Gail. You go ahead. I will take care of your students. They can come to my room. OK?"

"Lucy?" Gail asks, wanting to pursue the previous matter.

"It's nothing, Gail. Really." Somehow Gail feels that Lucy is being evasive.

"What is going on?" Gail murmurs as she walks toward the elevator. "Has Lucy not been honest with me?"

Moments later Gail enters Dr. Reed's office, her face flushed. Dr. Reed and Cheryl Rossman are there along with a parent.

Dr. Reed stands as she enters. "Miss Simons, this is Mrs. Rogers." Gail extends her hand as Dr. Reed continues. Gail remembers that the parent she saw earlier wore the same red coat. "Mrs. Rogers has a daughter in your A.P. class named Camelia. She has shown us Camelia's term paper for which you assigned her a seventy. Is that right?"

"Yes. That's right," Gail answers.

"Mrs. Rossman and I have not had an opportunity to read the paper in its entirety. This is the first time we've seen it. What Mrs. Rogers wants to know is why her daughter received a seventy."

Gail can feel Mrs. Rogers' eyes start at her feet and move upward. "Well, one of the things I explained to Camelia was that I gave her a seventy because I felt parts of the paper were plagiarized."

Mrs. Rogers sits very straight and looks at Gail out of the corner of her eye. "I want you to know that my daughter spent hours working on this paper. In fact, I helped her with it. I know it is not plagiarized."

"Did you check any of her sources?" Cheryl Rossman asks Gail.

"No, I just have not had time. It appears that her sources aren't valid." Gail states. "But, as I said, because I have not had the time to check all of her sources, I have given her the benefit of the doubt and assigned her a seventy."

"I think she deserves a better grade than seventy! There's not a single red mark on the paper, so what did you take off for except the fact that you think she copied her paper out of a book? You have no proof of that!" Mrs. Rogers raises her voice.

"I used to be a librarian, Mrs. Rogers. I have read many books. I have every reason to believe that your daughter's paper was copied from a resource text, verbatim." Gail can feel the back of her neck becoming warm. She bites the corner of her bottom lip as she looks at the paper Dr. Reed holds in his hand.

"I know my daughter did not copy the paper from a book because I saw her note cards! She had everything written out on note cards. She wrote her paper directly from the note cards."

"Well," Dr. Reed begins. "I really don't see that . . ."

"Another thing I don't understand," Mrs. Rogers adds, "Why didn't you tell my daughter earlier that you felt her paper was plagiarized? This is exactly the same paper she turned in as her rough draft. Why have you waited until the end of the term to try to fail my daughter?"

"I don't grade rough drafts," Gail states.

Dr. Reed stands in order to bring the conference to a close. "Mrs. Rogers, why don't you allow Mrs. Rossman and me to take a look at this paper and see if we feel it is plagiarized? We will get back with you tomorrow."

Mrs. Rogers rises. She is not as tall as Gail, but much larger in stature. "I don't intend to create problems, Dr. Reed, but I do a lot of substitute teaching throughout this school system and I know what goes on. I do not want my daughter unduly penalized because of mere conjuncture. I want my daughter to get an athletic scholarship so she can attend college and this will hurt her chances."

"We appreciate your coming in to talk to us, Mrs. Rogers. We will definitely get back in touch with you in a few days."

Gail looks up at the clock and notices that it is half past seven. "I have just a few minutes remaining to review my students for their exam. May I be excused?"

"Yes, Miss Simmons, go ahead. Mrs. Rossman and I will get back with you."

Gail is happy that Mrs. Rogers is walking toward her car by the time she exit's the main office. She certainly does not wish to be confronted outside of the office. Gail realizes, however, that Camelia will be sitting in her classroom for more than two hours today because of exams. She wonders how to respond to Camelia.

Two hours later Cheryl enters Gail's room and summons Camelia to the office. Gail notices the encyclopedia that Cheryl has tucked under her arm. Her characteristic smile is missing. There is a worried look in her luminous eyes.

Moments later, the door opens and Cheryl reappears, still carrying the encyclopedia. She lays the encyclopedia on Gail's desk and opens it, placing Camelia's term paper beside it.

"Dr. Reed and I compared what is in this encyclopedia with Camelia's paper and they are identical." She places a slightly clenched fist on her side, causing one side of her tailored suit coat to move toward the back. Gail can feel Cheryl's eyes watching her closely.

"Oh, yeah," Gail says softly. "This is what I was afraid of." She flips several pages and compares them with the term paper. "This is why I gave her a seventy."

"It looks like her whole paper is taken from this book," Gail continues. "She hasn't used any other sources at all, has she?"

"Obviously not," Cheryl answers. "Dr. Reed and I have contacted Mrs. Rogers and reported what we have found. She wants her daughter to be given an opportunity to do the paper over, but we don't have much time. So, I don't know. What do you think?"

"It doesn't matter to me," Gail answers. "The important thing to me is that she learns how to write a term paper before she graduates."

"Well, Dr. Reed and I feel the same way. If it is all right with you, I will work with her and make sure she follows procedures. I certainly feel that she is going to have difficulty getting through college if she doesn't learn how to write a term paper. And if you don't have time to grade it, I will be more than happy to do that, too."

"That sounds reasonable to me," Gail states, happy to have the matter resolved. The metallic ringing of the bell interrupts their thoughts momentarily and sends the students racing out into the hallways eager to socialize.

"One thing we need to discuss, however, is your treatment of the students' rough drafts. Dr. Reed and I both feel that, in the future, all rough drafts are to be carefully graded, including note cards. A student's graded rough draft should serve as a model for the final draft. OK?"

"Yeah. I realize that now," Gail says, softly.

"One way to avoid situations like this from occurring in the future is to spend time reviewing those rough drafts carefully. The rough draft is the vehicle through which the student learns to write a polished product. Camelia really doesn't deserve the seventy you gave her. So, what I will tell her is that if she wants to receive the seventy, she must submit another paper. Is that fair enough?"

"Oh, there you are," Mrs. Easley states as the door swings open. "You are just the two people I need to see." She immediately sits at a student desk, obviously out of breath.

"We have a problem surfacing that I think we need to nip in the bud right away." She has a hand full of forms that she spreads out on the desk where she sits.

"Three students came by my room just this moment asking me to sign for them to come back to my class in January. I know you're not aware of this Mrs. Rossman, but I have taken four already because the counselor said their parents were quite adamant."

Gail watches Cheryl closely as the furrows in her brow grow deeper and her luminous eyes get larger. Cheryl moves closer to Mrs. Easley and peers over her shoulder to look at the forms.

"Now, I'm willing to do whatever you and Dr. Reed want me to do." Mrs. Easley continues, "I think you know that. I will teach fifty students at one time if that's what you want. I don't think they will learn as much if I have to grade fifty term papers every week instead of twenty, but I will do my best."

"What is going on, Mrs. Easley?" Cheryl asks.

"It appears that the students are comparing notes. If they are not covering the exact same material in Miss Simmons' class that my students are covering, they assume that they will be doomed when they get to college."

"Aren't the two of you covering the same material?" Cheryl asks. She looks at Gail and then at Mrs. Easley, waiting for a response.

Gail feels her throat tighten. She knows that she should answer, but she can't. She opens her mouth to speak, but the words won't come. She knows how she has avoided Mrs. Easley for weeks, hoping that she wouldn't discover how far behind her students are.

Mrs. Easley breaks the silence. "Now, I'll be honest with you, Cheryl. I have not made it a point to check behind Gail every week or so because she is a professional just as I am. I know she will come to me if she has any questions. You know, I just do not feel comfortable looking over her shoulder. It just doesn't seem ethical. She has to be given professional license to teach the class as she deems appropriate." Mrs. Easley tilts her head upward and peers underneath her glasses.

"My question is simply this," Mrs. Easley continues. "Should we allow these students to change or not?"

"We'd better not," Cheryl says. "Let me take those and I will meet with the counselor." Cheryl takes the schedule change forms which Mrs. Easley holds in her direction.

"Well, I'm glad you made that decision," Mrs. Easley states. "I don't think we need to let them have their way. The next thing you know they'll be trying to tell us what to teach." She chuckles softly as she and Cheryl walk out together.

Gail is happy that she can breathe again. She feels as if she has held her breath for the last fifteen minutes. She looks at the mound of exams she has to grade and is thankful that the second exam period is her planning time. She takes a long, deep breath and tackles those papers with a vengeance.

Gail tries desperately to avoid thinking about the events of the day. She is thankful that she can immerse herself in the work that has to be done in order to close the semester. Through tear-filled eyes she grades exams, records grades, makes out yellow course cards, distributes those cards to the appropriate teachers and begins the cycle all over again. By the end of the day her trembling hands are red and blistered.

The work is agonizingly slow, but Gail plods along. By Thursday night she realizes that the workload is too overwhelming. She decides to call Rosie.

"Hi Gail," Rosie's husband answers. "How in the world are you?"

Gail doesn't talk to him often, but she wonders why he is speaking so low. "I'm sinking," Gail answers. "The paperwork is killing me. And tomorrow is our deadline, you know."

"Yeah. I know. I helped Rosie finish hers up this afternoon. I felt so sorry for her. She's come down with a bad case of this flu that's going around."

"Oh, no! Don't tell me that! Does she feel like talking to me for a minute?"

"Well, she's asleep right now. I'll have her call you when she wakes up. She really feels lousy."

Gail hangs the phone up with a thud. Somehow she knows that Rosie will not call tonight, and tomorrow will be too late. She rubs her stomach in an attempt to soothe the gnawing pain. The feeling is all too familiar. She wonders how many ulcers she has developed in the last few months.

The loneliness creeps in and envelopes Gail like a cloak of darkness. The mound of papers in front of her fades in and out as she struggles to maintain composure in the face of an insurmountable task. By 2:00 a.m. she resigns herself to staying up for the remainder of the night. The ticking of the clock begins to sound faint. Her eyes become heavy and her shoulders weaken under the strain. No matter how hard she tries, sleep finally overtakes her.

When she first hears it she thinks she's dreaming. Then she hears it again. She sits up, peers at her watch and peels herself away from the kitchen chair. This time she's certain the ringing she hears is the doorbell.

"Who could possibly be ringing my doorbell at 4:00 a.m.?" she asks herself as she races to the bathroom and splashes her face with cold water. As she moves toward the door she hears a voice she recognizes.

"I'm dreaming of a white Christmas! Just like the one we used to knowww..."

Gail opens the door. There is so much snow that she has trouble focusing.

"Jeff! What in the world are you doing out at this hour?"

Jeff looks more handsome than ever. A brown, wool cap covers most of his blond hair, which is neatly trimmed. His clear, blue eyes look into

Gail's, longingly. His glistening white teeth bring a ray of sunshine to the gloomy clouds beckoning the unexpected winter storm.

"Aren't you gonna' invite the snowman inside, princess?"

"Yes! Yes, of course. Come on in, Jeff. You must be freezing."

"Not anymore." He moves inside, catches Gail around her waist and pulls her close.

"I've missed you, Gail. I couldn't stay away any longer. I had to see you."

Moments later the explanations and apologies come easier and all the rough places are made smooth again. Gail cannot imagine having fun grading the few papers which remain. But, in time, the papers get graded and the grades get recorded in a jovial, light atmosphere that only Jeff seems to make happen for her.

The bumpy ride to Melrose in Jeff's jeep is more fun than a sleigh ride. The snow has fallen without warning and doesn't appear to be slowing down. The trees surrounding Melrose appear stark beneath the blanket of fresh snow.

As Jeff leaves the parking lot, Gail waves until the Jeep is hidden by the swirling snow. Her hands do not tremble as she signs in and places a mound of course grade cards in teachers' mailboxes. She smiles and greets every person she meets.

"Gail, about that A.P. class. I only meant. . ."

"Lucy, it's OK. You don't have to explain. I understand. You really did me a favor." The perplexed look in Lucy's eyes causes Gail to continue. "But that's what a true friend is for. Right?"

They are interrupted by Dr. Reed's announcement. "Due to the inclement weather conditions, we will be on an abbreviated schedule today. As soon as your grades are submitted, you are free to go home. I wish everyone a Merry Christmas and a Happy New Year!"

"Happy New Year, Lucy!" Gail whispers as she hugs her neck and walks swiftly down the vacant corridor.

A sparkling Christmas tree stands in the reception area right outside Cheryl's office. Christmas carols are playing softly on a radio and the aroma of hot spiced tea fills the air.

Cheryl's door is almost always open, so Gail walks in without knocking. Cheryl is seated at her desk looking at a computer printout and smiling to herself. Her smile broadens when she sees Gail.

"Hello, Gail. Merry Christmas!"

"And Merry Christmas to you, Mrs. Rossman," She sits at the conference table in her usual place and waits for Cheryl to join her. She watches the snow as it swirls against the glass door. The flakes are larger than ever now.

"Well, the semester is almost over. Do you need any help with anything? I know this has been a difficult time for you. It's difficult for all of us at the close of the semester, so I know it has been doubly hard for you." Gail reads a genuineness in Cheryl's eyes.

"No, thank you. I managed to get through it, somehow." She feels a tightness in her throat. When she clears her throat, the tightness remains.

"Well, I want you to know that I really appreciate your participation in my research project. I realize it was a time-consuming process which required quite a commitment. We will only need to have one interview during the spring, though, and then a final group interview with my major professor from the university."

There is a long pause. "So, what are your plans for the Christmas holidays?" Cheryl asks.

"Well, I think I'll sleep for about a month." They both laugh.

"Don't sleep quite that long. You'll miss out on the beginning of the spring semester."

Gail looks down at the piece of frayed carpet with which she feels a kinship. It seems more fragile than ever now, as if a vacuum cleaner has yanked yet another thread from its base. "That's what I wanted to talk to you about," she begins.

Cheryl's large eyes look into Gail's, waiting patiently for her to continue. "I have decided that . . . I will not be back next semester." Cheryl's eyes soften.

Neither of them speaks for a moment. At last Gail says, "I've given it a lot of thought . . . and I don't think I'm cut out to be a teacher." She waits for Cheryl to speak, but she says nothing.

Gail swallows hard and continues. "I can't keep suffering this way. It's just too hard." She lets out a long, deep sigh like so many times before when she has sat across the table from Cheryl.

"I understand," Cheryl says, very softly. "Have you told Dr. Reed?"

"I didn't know exactly how I should do this. That's why I wanted to talk to you first."

"We will need an official letter of resignation. But you have some time. There's no need to rush."

"No, I'd like to get this over with. I will put my letter in the mail tomorrow." Gail feels the heavy burden gradually lifting from her shoulders as she stands to leave.

"So what will you do?" Cheryl asks.

"I don't really know," Gail says softly. "I will figure something out." She looks out the glass door at the swiftly falling snow and wonders how she will get home. She knows she should call Jeff to let him know she is leaving early.

"Well, I hate to see you go, but I hope you know that you have a lot of other talents and abilities that can be used in so many other areas."

"Thank you."

Cheryl moves closer and touches her on the shoulder. "I also want you to know that I will help you in any way I can. All you have to do is let me know."

"You have helped me so much, already." Gail can no longer look in Cheryl's direction.

"You will keep in touch, then?"

"Yes. I will." Gail moves toward the glass door.

"Oh, Gail! Wait a moment! I almost forgot to share the good news with you. You remember the Proficiency Test that your students took in November?"

Gail closes the door and moves back inside. "Yes. Yes, I do." The warmth envelopes her like a cloak.

"Well," Cheryl's eyes sparkle with excitement. "You will be pleased to know that eighteen of your twenty-four students passed! Isn't that wonderful?"

"Not bad," Gail says with a smile. Not bad."

Gail opens the door leading from Cheryl's office once more and allows it to close behind her. The cold snowflakes land on the bridge of her nose and turn to gentle rain. She almost turns back as she struggles to walk against the wind.

Thought Questions

Chapter 9 – Against the Wind

1. What surprises do Gail face in this chapter?

2. How do you feel about Gail's decision to resign?

3. What good news does Gail learn in this chapter?

4. What do you feel really happened to Gail in her first year of teaching?

5. What do you feel could have saved her from leaving the profession?

6. What changes do we need to make in our preservice training and treatment of new teachers?

Chapter 10

TEACHABLE MOMENTS

"Mr. DeLoach," Cheryl says, "we would like for you to come in tomorrow for orientation and to review the materials needed for all of your classes. We will arrange for the substitute to take your classes for three or four days until you feel you're prepared."

Don DeLoach's face mirrors his agreement with the proposed schedule. "You mean I don't have to take over the classes today?"

"Do you feel you are prepared to do that, today?" Cheryl asks.

"No. But it has never made a difference in the past. I must tell you that I am extremely grateful to be given some time to get prepared. How is it that you were able to convince personnel to cover those classes with a substitute for three or four days?"

"Well," Cheryl states, rather proud of her accomplishment, "sometimes you just have to let them know that you're serious about supporting your staff."

"Well, I've been around a long time and this is the first time ever that I've had an appreciable amount of time to get prepared. You must be a new breed as far as principals are concerned."

"Let's just say I've learned some valuable lessons along the way," says Cheryl with a far-away look in her luminous eyes as her thoughts turn back to Gail Simmons.

Don DeLoach leans back in his chair and looks at Cheryl across the conference table. Somehow, Cheryl knows that he senses there is a story behind her words. Cheryl realizes that Don is no stranger to education. He has served as a teacher and principal in Egypt and has also taught at a school for juvenile delinquents. He has developed a keen sensitivity to the feelings of others.

His short-cropped hair which is combed to the front reminds her of the pictures of Julius Caesar she has seen in literature books. He has a glass eye that stares motionlessly, but a compassion that comes through with his every word.

"Tell me about these students, Mrs. Rossman, and what kind of experience they have had so far this year. You and I both know how much of a challenge it can be to take a group of students in mid-year and move them in the right direction without a real struggle," Mr. DeLoach remaks.

"I agree that it can be tough, Mr. DeLoach. But I think the important thing for you is to go in with a winning attitude and prepared to respond to their concerns and needs. And that's what you and I are going to explore for the next few days. What are these students' needs? And what are their concerns likely to be? Does that sound fair enough, Mr. DeLoach?"

"Yes, ma'am it does."

"Then, let's get started." Cheryl clears her throat and picks up the phone.

"How do you like your coffee, Mr. DeLoach?" she asks as she dials her secretary's number. Within moments, hot coffee arrives and Don DeLoach's official orientation to his new assignment at Melrose begins.

By the end of the first day Don DeLoach has met each administrator and all office staff. He has been introduced to the custodian, the cafeteria manager, each department head, every member of the English department, and received an extensive tour of the building. In addition, the English teacher across the hall from his room has been assigned the responsibility of serving as his mentor.

He spends two full days perusing textbooks and materials pertinent to his assigned classes and making out lesson plans for the first week. Much of his time is spent in the school library uncovering resources and taking advantage of the expertise of the media specialists.

He spends a final day talking to the substitute and unobtrusively observing several of the classes. By the end of the fourth day, Cheryl feels that he is prepared to assume full responsibility for his assigned classes. One request he makes of Cheryl, however, is that he swap the A.P. class with another teacher who has taught English at the school for a while.

"You may consider me strange, Mrs. Rossman," he explains. "But I prefer to work with low achievers. I get quite a bit of satisfaction out of seeing them accomplish more than they ever thought they could. My experience in Egypt and with the juvenile court system has really taught me some valuable lessons about the disadvantaged." He maintains eye contact while he talks.

"I do enjoy teaching the academic achiever, but it's just I feel the low achiever needs me more. The academic achiever is going to make it with or without me, but the slow learner may not make it without my help. I think I know how to help them." Don explains.

"And how is that?" Cheryl asks.

"Believing in them and helping them to believe in themselves. That's the key." There is a sincerity in his demeanor that Cheryl likes.

Cheryl moves on his request and in doing so makes two teachers very happy, namely, Mr. DeLoach and the teacher who receives the A.P. class.

Cheryl is determined to be unrelenting in her efforts to provide all the help that Mr. DeLoach needs. She talks honestly about her plans on the day before Mr. DeLoach meets his students.

"Don, I've really enjoyed these last four days and I can see that you have accomplished a great deal. I feel very good about your readiness to take on full teaching responsibilities, at this point." She weighs her words very carefully, so as not to offend.

"I hope that you will not mind my hovering close to you for the next few days. One of the things I would like to do is to introduce you to each class and explain that you will be their teacher for the remainder of the year. Another thing I would like to do is to stay in the classroom with you for a day or two just to assist you when you need it."

"That sounds fine with me, Mrs. Rossman. You're the boss."

Cheryl thinks of Gail quite often and accepts part of the responsibility for her departure from the profession. She doesn't feel good about what transpired. She only feels remorseful. She feels a deep sense of guilt for having contributed to Gail's demise.

Cheryl proudly introduces Mr. DeLoach to the students in first period and anxiously waits to see how his first day is going to develop. She knows how critical a smooth first day is to continued success in his classroom. She occupies a seat in the cramped room and observes Mr. DeLoach in action.

To Cheryl, he appears rather mild mannered and not easily rattled by events. He carefully explains to his students what his experience has been for the past few years. He talks openly about Egypt and the youngsters he has taught in the juvenile institution. He then focuses his attention on his students in a way that makes Cheryl's heart sing.

"So you came back from your Christmas vacation and you saw a strange name on your schedule card," he begins, walking up and down each aisle with his arms folded comfortably. "What did you think?" There is silence. "Come on. Say it. I can take it." There is more silence. He grabs his roll book and selects a name. "What did you think, Reginald?"

"Nothing."

"John? What about you?"

"All I thought about was fresh meat!"

"Oh, I see. So you just knew that you had another opportunity to do a teacher in. Right?"

"Right on!" John says. The class laughs.

"I'm fresh meat to you. I'll accept that. Your role is to whip me into shape. Am I right, Lance?" He selects another name at random.

"I wouldn't go that far, Sir," Lance states.

"So, how would you describe this situation, then? How would you describe this new relationship we've entered into?" The students listen intently, trying to determine where this strange, new teacher is coming from.

There is more silence. "Didn't any of you attempt to check me out? Find out what I was like?"

A youngster in the back raises his hand. He removes his cap simultaneously.

"Yes?" Mr. DeLoach responds.

"Yeah, but nobody knew."

"Ok. So, what happens when nobody knows a person's track record?"

"You make assumptions," Lance volunteers.

"Absolutely!" Don Deloach responds. "It's like going on a blind date. You imagine what the guy or gal is going to be like and look like; what kind of personality he or she has. Right?"

"She better have fine legs!" Joe says. The class roars with laughter.

Don DeLoach pivots and moves swiftly back to the front of the room to make his point. "So, you do have expectations built up. And if someone doesn't live up to them, then. . . ." A hand is raised. "Reginald?"

"You're let down," Reginald says with confidence.

"Right, you're let down." He grabs a piece of chalk from the blackboard. "Now, you have expectations of me and I have expectations of you. And what we are going to do today is talk about those expectations. Because it's best to get them out in the open so we will know what they are."

He draws a vertical line down the middle of the board. "We're going to start with me first. On one side, we will list the expectations you have of me and on the other side we will list the expectations I have of you." He looks at the students carefully, seeking their full attention. "Is that fair enough?"

"That's cool!" Joe says at a much lower volume than usual.

"Now. What are your expectations of me? You talk and I'll write." He places one hand on the blackboard and faces the class. He sees a female student's hand go up on the front row. "Yes?"

"The first thing I look for is when the teacher comes in and everyone is talking real loud and you say get quiet and everyone keeps talking and you don't say anything. You don't want to take control of the class, and no one wants to give you control. On the other hand, if you come in class and say be quiet and when we keep talking you say I mean get quiet. I will want to give you respect. So, I expect you to get control of the class and make us get quiet."

"OK. Well said. So number one on this side of the board will be To have control of the class." He writes very legibly and straight.

"What is another expectation that you have of your teachers?" Students begin to speak quite freely now.

"You can just tell by the way they come in how you're supposed to act. The way they move, what they do, how they control the paperwork, you know. Like, some teachers lose your work. When a teacher loses your work you know that this teacher is not in control of her own life, so you can take control of the class."

Don DeLoach paraphrases each statement before recording it on the board. "So, expectation number two is To be organized and stay on top of the paperwork. Next?"

The same student continues. "That's just real important to show me that. Because I know some teachers around here I don't expect a whole lot out of because you go to class and you ask may we get those papers back from the test we took three weeks ago and they say something like, 'I haven't finished'. That's no control! A teacher should be able to grade anything in three weeks."

"OK. Let's go to another expectation," Mr. DeLoach says. Cheryl is absolutely astonished at their candid answers. She wishes she had remembered to bring her tape recorder.

Another female voice responds. "Some teachers, you know, don't come to class on time, yet they expect us to. Like, I have this teacher who is always out in the hall talking to her male friends instead of teaching her class. And I also have this teacher who is always doing something else, like basketball."

"So expectation number three is <u>To report to class on time and care about student learning</u>."

"Yes," she responds.

"OK, what is expectation number four? Anyone."

A young man responds. "Attitude, too! Some teachers have negative attitudes! Well, I had a teacher who, from the very beginning, had a negative attitude toward people and stuff. And every time you look up she's trying to confront somebody about something. And like if somebody was to say something to her, you know, she has a nasty attitude in what she has to say. That makes me mad! So I decided that I was going to act the same way she was acting."

"OK. So expectation number four is <u>To exhibit a positive attitude</u>." He writes on the board and spies another hand raised in the middle. "Go right ahead."

This time the student is a rather robust female. "Yeah. It's good to go by the rules, but when you just go strictly by the rules then that's not going to get it. If you're going to be too strict, that's dumb. A teacher has to know when to ease up." She pops her gum and continues.

"Some teachers got so many rules that you can't do anything in class. Rules aren't bad. I'm not against rules, but you can have too many rules. Like you can't chew gum, you can't turn around, you can't talk the whole period, you can't do this; you can't do that. And you sit there, and they ask you to stay awake in class. I mean, it's literally impossible, especially if you just have to read a book or something."

Don DeLoach ponders for a moment. He abandons one piece of chalk for another. "I think I hear two assumptions in your response. One is for teachers <u>To be flexible but strict, and another is To make learning interesting and fun</u>. Am I right?"

"Right."

"OK. We have six expectations up here. Is this it? Is this all you're going to expect from me? Think long and hard because this is your one chance to tell me how you expect me to behave. You're next."

Cheryl is sure those students aren't going to let him get by that easily. She smiles as another hand goes up.

The young man wears a suit and tie, deviating from the traditional uniform. "To be nice is good, and I think teachers should be nice. But when someone skips class and you don't do anything about it, I mean, you gotta set an example every now and then. You can let students go so far until they just get over on you. If a teacher doesn't control his own classroom, then the students are going to think it's all right to just keep on breaking rules."

"So, what you want is for teachers <u>To establish rules and set boundaries, as well as consequences for breaking the rules?</u>"

"Absolutely. They need to enforce the rules."

"OK, class, you're doing well. We're up to eight expectations now. Are there any others? You think that's enough?" He scans the room and waits. Cheryl is absolutely captivated.

"Well," a young man in the back row begins, "some teachers feel like they don't have to give students any respect. Some teachers hold grades over your head, you know. They say if you don't do what I say, then, you don't get a decent grade. And no matter how well you do, they won't give you what you really deserve."

"Yeah!" Several students agree.

"All I expect from a teacher is if I give them respect, for them to give me respect." The class applauds.

Cheryl watches as Don DeLoach remains unaffected by the applause. He doesn't take issue with any of their comments. He simply facilitates the process and clarifies issues. "I think I've heard two different expectations again," he comments. "Tell me if I'm wrong, now. Number nine is <u>To treat students fairly</u> and number ten is <u>To give students respect</u>."

The young man crosses his legs and shakes his head, "There you go! That's it!"

"OK. Look at your list carefully. Have you left anything out? It looks like a pretty extensive list to me. And I think I can live up to your expectations." He lays the piece of chalk on the tray and faces the class. "You've done well. Now, let's move. . ."

A young female student interrupts, "There's one thing that really upsets me."

"OK, lets' hear it."

"It's like, you get in the classroom and you be playing around, and the teacher won't say anything. He just doesn't have control of his classroom. He's teaching, and there's other people disrupting on purpose, you know, distracting. And it's, like, he ignores them. It's like, the noise is not there and he keeps on teaching and teaching. And you say to yourself, 'Aww, I got this teacher made.' So, you just give that teacher a hard time."

Don DeLoach looks at the board. "All right. Thank you. Is there anything up there already that covers that area?"

The student looks at the board pensively, with her chin held against a clenched fist, her elbow resting on her desk. "Yeah. I think the first one will get it. The one about having control of the class."

"Yeah, I think so, too," Don DeLoach says. "You all have done a superb job. I will jot this list down and read it ever so often, so I won't have any problems sticking to your expectations."

He pauses and looks at the board again, pivots, and picks up a fresh piece of chalk. "Now, let's move to the other side of the board. My list of expectations of you is not as long as yours, but it's just as important to our being able to get along well together and learn." He watches their faces carefully to make sure they are listening and understanding.

"I only have five expectations of you, and I want you to get out a sheet of paper and write these down." Notebooks open and close and book bags move up and down. Several students go to the pencil sharpener. During the transition, Don DeLoach walks up and down the aisles.

"Is everyone ready?" There is silence. "OK, my five expectations are these." He begins to write, but verbalizes at the same time, "To come to class on time; To always be prepared; To respect the rights of others; To follow the rules of the school; and To follow classroom rules."

"Now, you all know what the school rules are. Right? And you know if you do not follow those rules you can get into serious trouble." He begins to walk up and down the aisles again while some students finish writing. Some students swing around in their seats so they can watch him and catch his every word.

"One thing we don't have, though, is a set of classroom rules." He removes a pencil from behind his ear momentarily and replaces it. "In other words, how should you conduct yourselves while in our classroom?" He pauses, but not long enough for them to answer.

"We're not going to answer this question today, because we're out of time. What I want you to do, though, is to come prepared tomorrow to formulate a set of classroom rules that all of you should follow." He moves to the front of the room again and paces.

"Now, I already know what I think our classroom rules should be, but you see, this classroom doesn't just belong to me. It belongs to all of us. So, together, we will develop a set of classroom rules that we all can live with. I'll be able to put some of my rules up on the board and you will be able to put some of your rules up on the board. Is that fair enough?"

There is silence. "Yeah. That's cool. That's real cool!" John says, just as the bell rings.

The throng of students leave surrounded by the usual chatter, but today there seems to be something different in their mood. Several students offer Don DeLoach a handshake, but most of them want to take a closer look at this newcomer to Melrose.

"Don, that was brilliant!" Cheryl says with a smile. "Is this the way you always meet a new group of students?"

"The one thing I always try to accomplish with my group of students," he says, "is to create the teachable moment. If I can create the teachable moment for each of my classes, then I will have done my job."

"Well, Don," Cheryl says with a sparkle in her luminous eyes, "there is no doubt in my mind that you will create a room full of teachable moments every day. Welcome to the Rose!"

As Cheryl walks around toward another classroom, deeply impressed by what she has observed, she bumps into Joey Miller. "Joey," she says, "tell me something?"

"Sure, Mrs. Rossman. Anything."

"Why is it that students give some teachers a hard time, but not others?"

Joey peers at Cheryl Rossman, looks at his watch, and gives her that crooked smile. "Are you serious, Mrs. Rossman?" he asks.

"I guess not, Joey. I guess not. That's another research question altogether. It can wait. You'd better go on to class so you won't be late."

"Thank you, Mrs. Rossman. You're cool!" He scampers off to class, determined to beat the bell. As he disappears around the corner, Cheryl wonders when would be an appropriate time to get a group of students together to pursue that question.

She shakes her head, knowing that she already has enough to keep her busy for the next twenty years. Even now, she's on her way to check on Lucy Cummings, Laura Perkins, Patsy Miller, Roxanne Baker, and Clyde Reynolds, the other fresh roses teaching at Melrose for the first time this year. She takes a deep breath and says to herself, "Never stop caring, Cheryl Rossman. Never stop caring."

Thought Questions

Chapter 10 – Teachable Moments

1. What differences do you see in Gail Simmons' induction into Melrose and the induction of Don DeLoach?

2. If Don DeLoach and Gail Simmons were to change places in this story, what do you feel would have happened?

3. What prediction can you make about Don Deloach's future in education?

4. What advice can you give to newcomers to school organizations?

5. What advice can you give to school administrators as they welcome newcomers to their schools each year?

6. What are your takeaways from this novel?

The Purple Rose

Dan Dammann

The roots go down, the flower goes up. Nobody knows why.
Roses don't root well in autumn.
They struggle through winter.
This rose still lives; a rose unique is trussed.
Picture, if you will, a rose of laser purple,
delicate, regal.
It is hopeful in the ground, waiting its new awakening.
Fragile and delicate in anticipation of its waking, the rose
Dazzles in its new brilliance, wanting to be itself.
It stirs, opens, is drawn to the newness of the garden,
unlike any it has ever seen.
This royally, wondrous creation sees and breathes and sighs
in the newfound garden, much too big to be noticed.
Other roses are there, the soil seems fertile, the budding
sprouts its fresh newness.
The gardener gently waters this marvelous, new beginning as
the autumn colors changes their hue.
The rose is; the rose isn't. The rose can't see its
brilliant hue or touch its petals. Feel?
It's hard to be fragile in the coming winds of cold. Please
accept me in your ground so rich. Cold.
The autumn foliage returns to ground and a noble creature of
nature's handiwork sips the chill of winter's freeze.
The cooling winds of fall foretell the arrival of harsh
days. Will they be days of ice? Snow? Growth?
The gardeners do not notice, the soil threatens, the warm
glow of past sunlight dulls;
The newfound wonder, discovered at its awakening, turns to
fear and dread.
The joy of raindrop sprays no longer freshen as the wilting
grows each day and hour.
"No one knows," it seems to say to anyone who will hear.
"I'm lost and the rain has turned to tears.
Who am I? What am I? Where have I been? What will I be?

Does anyone hear or see?
Does anybody care? It must be me. I know it's me. I am
withered, spent and lost."
The other flowers, fresh and grown as well see not. The
wilting of the infant rose is concealed,
The time is now, indeed, it is no more; for the regal
rose of newness is transformed. Forget you not,
Purple, Vivid Rose.

AFTERWORD

This research project on teachers as newcomers was completed in the spring of 1989. Gail Simmons was the only member of the group of participants who left before the end of the school year.

Although each of the six case studies revealed features of the socialization process which were problematic, Gail Simmons' case uncovered a larger and more complex array of problems. My interest in forcing the reader to respond and face the realities of teaching in an unfamiliar organization was one factor considered in focusing on this worst case scenario. Hopefully, this focus will increase the reader's awareness of the problems faced by newcomers to school organizations and generate interest in developing appropriate interventions.

Although the nature of each subject's socialization was strongly influenced by the organization, certainly differences in the personalities and personal influences of the subjects made a difference in their response to the situations they faced. Gail's lack of a well-formulated philosophy of teaching was certainly a major contributor to her demise. Her desire to teach was based upon her devotion to her family and her need to preserve a family tradition. Thus, her familiarity with teaching gave her a false sense of security. When she faced her own classroom, the familiar felt strange.

Gail also lacked a realistic picture of the teaching art. Her observation of teachers and brief experience had left her with the impression that teaching was relatively easy and unencumbered. Her level of reality shock was more pronounced than the other subjects, although her teaching assignment was no more complex than that of Laura Perkins.

Laura, the beginning teacher who arrived near the end of the first six weeks, encountered difficulties comparable to those experienced by Gail Simmons. She, too, was assigned low achievers and multiple preparations. In addition, she had no classroom of her own. Laura persevered, however, making office referrals when appropriate and seeking the help and advice of her colleagues. Determined to learn from her mistakes, she returned the following year and created a more positive classroom climate. At the writing of this novel, she is in her fourth year at Melrose and is a definite success story.

After her first year, Laura rarely made an office referral, was a strong disciplinarian, and was highly respected by her students and colleagues. She served as Teacher Association Building Representative for two years and was viewed as a key player within the school. She actively sought professional and personal development opportunities and has continued to provide a rich and varied instructional program even in the face of student resistance. Lastly, she has maintained her enthusiasm for teaching although she has sometimes felt battered and discouraged.

Of the three beginning teachers, Patsy Miller had the smoothest transition and the most successful first year. She had spent the previous year engaged in student teaching at Melrose so her prior knowledge and understanding of the school culture made a distinct difference. Another factor is that Patsy was assigned only one preparation and the students were average ability level. The following year she agreed to teach a subject for which she was ill-prepared in order to maintain her position at Melrose. Sadly, she encountered much difficulty and her classroom management skills deteriorated, causing her confidence to plummet. Patsy is now teaching at a middle school.

Clyde Reynolds, who was new to the system, requested a transfer to another school due to a disagreement with the administration. After an eight year career change, he had come back to teaching with high expectations. He was hopeful that parents were more involved in the education of their children and that student apathy was lower. After one semester, however, Clyde perceived that students and schools had worsened significantly during the period of time he had worked in other occupations. He experienced a high level of reality shock comparable to that experienced by the beginning teachers.

The other two experienced teachers, Roxanne Baker and Lucy Cummings, both had a reasonably successful year and, at the time this novel was written, were still teaching at Melrose. Their recent experience in neighboring schools served to ameliorate the negative effects of their new status. They experienced very low levels of reality shock. Experience tended to mediate the stress related to being new because those teachers could anticipate events. Teachers who came back to the occupation after an extended absence of from eight to twelve years, however, felt that starting over was almost like being brand new to the field.

All of the newcomers, with the exception of Don DeLoach, experienced various levels of reality shock. Don experienced the smoothest transition and encountered fewer problems than any other member of the group. His prior experience, the concentrated amount of orientation time he received, and the nurturing relationship he developed with a willing mentor were contributing factors.

So we see that just as individuals may become differently socialized because of differences in the structure of the social settings in which they interact, so may they become differently socialized because of differences in past experience, motivations, and capabilities. The following vignette regarding the six case study participants substantiates this tendency.

The six case study subjects represented a broad cross-section of abilities and experience. Of the three experienced teachers, two of the subjects were new-to-the-building and one was new-to-the-system. Those subjects who were new-to-the-building appeared to encounter fewer adjustment problems because of their familiarity with the school system and knowledge of current teaching trends. The subject who was new-to-the-system seemed to encounter as many adjustment problems as the beginning teachers because of idealistic expectations.

The subjects' predominant adjustment strategy appeared to be strategic compliance (Lacey, 1977; Zeichner & Tabachnick, 1983). All of the subjects reacted strongly against the constraints posed in the school, but because of the nature of the constraints and because of their low status as newcomers, they generally acted in ways demanded by the situation while maintaining strong reservations about doing so. Two of the subjects chose to use strategic redefinition to adjust to the changes. The beginning teacher who selected strategic redefinition was successful at changing the status quo to a degree, but the experienced teacher was not. The experienced teacher who attempted strategic redefinition requested a transfer to another school. The one beginning teacher who was not successful at employing any of the social strategies resigned her position at mid-year to seek work in another occupation. Although two of the subjects chose to exit the organization, four of the subjects remained in the organization and managed to feel like insiders by the end of the year.

An analysis of these data revealed that four factors had significant influence on the teachers' abilities to adjust to the school culture: prior experience, day-to-day interactions with students, their work conditions, and interactions with colleagues and principals. In addition, adjustment problems experienced by the newcomers appeared to be associated with the following factors: student behavior, the absence of adequate orientation programs, the absence of visible signs of sustained support from the administration, the absence of a classroom of one's own, and pervasive isolation from colleagues. The most common problems cited by the respondents were discipline and classroom management, lack of time for planning and organizing, and motivating students. These findings are consistent with previous research findings (Cusick, 1983; Lortie, 1975; Jordell, 1987; Clark & Peterson, 1986; Veenman, 1984; Houston, 1988; Howey, 1989).

An analysis of the data reflects that both formal and informal means of socialization existed in the school organization. Formal means of socialization stemmed from the administration and included the interview, a tour, orientation, and evaluation.

The interview provided an opportunity for newcomers to be introduced to the history and lore of the school. During the interview, newcomers were questioned to determine how closely their beliefs matched the philosophy and goals of the school. In addition, extra-curricular and co-curricular assignments such as forensics coach, cheerleading sponsor, newspaper or annual sponsor were often presented as a condition of employment.

The teachers learned of their role by way of their teaching assignment, which was typically a difficult one comprised of low achievers, large classes, and inadequate space and equipment. Two of the newcomers were not assigned a room of their own, resulting in the necessity to move to five different rooms in the building to meet classes.

Orientation sessions typically lasted from one hour to a full day and primarily explained the hierarchy of the school and procedures for submitting various bureaucratic reports and forms. Although this was not the case at Melrose, 60% of the teachers surveyed in the system reported they received no formal orientation to their assigned schools. Instead, they were notified of their assignment, given a copy of the teacher handbook and taken directly to their classroom.

A tour was sometimes conducted as part of the orientation process. The tour familiarized the newcomers with their location in the school and usually included an introduction to assistant principals and department chairpersons.

The evaluation process represented another form of socialization in that newcomers were apprised of organizational and system-wide expectations while engaged in these procedures. Evaluation also provided a mechanism through which newcomers could obtain a stamp of approval from the administration.

Informal means of socialization emanated from colleagues and from within the classroom. Colleagues' efforts to assist the newcomers were restricted by time limitations and the structure of the school. No formal socializing agents were designated and rarely did anyone voluntarily take new members under their wings. Essentially, newcomers to the school organization learned the ropes by trial and error.

Further, the administration's explanations of how things were to be done were often inconsistent with the norms established by the group. Yet, norms were not well-established and accepted by the total group, so the rules differed from one group to the next. Thus, newcomers discovered that their classrooms provided more meaning to the school organization. As they interacted with their students on a day-to-day basis, the students became their primary socializing agents (Jordell, 1987; Lortie, 1975; Friebus, 1977; Zeichner, 1983; Dreeben, 1979).

Students answered many of the newcomers' questions about how things were done, arranged various hazing experiences, and established many of the norms of the school. It was through interacting with students, then, that school culture began to take shape and that rules began to evolve and gain clarity.

Essentially, these teachers in transition did not have the benefit of certain rites or ceremonies designed to cushion the disturbance or lessen the crisis resulting from the sudden change in their status. In actuality, an informal rule existed requiring that recruits and other newcomers pay their dues by being assigned the most difficult students and the worst working conditions. Individuals who succeed under these work conditions, such as Laura Perkins, complete their rite of passage into the teaching ranks and are highly regarded.

Although these teachers gained meaning primarily from interacting with students, they also derived some meaning from a few symbols in the workplace. A room of one's own, a symbol of great importance to the group, reflected that the teacher had been granted professional status. A room represented the domain where professionals practiced their craft and signaled that the teachers deserved respect in their own domain. Both subjects who moved from classroom to classroom suffered a lower self-concept and verbalized the feeling that students failed to accord them respect because they had no room to call their own.

Report cards were symbols of power used to reward students for their work or punish them for their failure to perform. The report card symbolized the teachers' power to provide a signal of approval or disapproval.

Tenure was a status symbol signaling that a teacher had joined the ranks as an accepted member of the profession. Teachers who had gained tenure had, for all practical purposes, paid their dues. Once teachers gained tenure they did not expect to be assigned the most difficult students or to teach without a classroom of their own. These expectations became an established norm which old-timers rigorously enforced.

There was some difference in the levels of professional concerns expressed by the case study subjects. Experienced participants expressed concern for the social and emotional needs of students, while beginning teachers' concerns related to their own survival and gaining mastery of the teaching task.

As has been the case in several other research studies (Ryan, 1970; Tisher, 1982; Murphy & Huling-Austin, 1987; Rosenholtz, et al., 1986), the socialization of teachers in this study was found to be highly context specific. Although the case study subjects worked at the same site, their experiences were different because they taught in three different departments, used different curricula, and responded to different sets of norms. This accounts, in part, for the differing socializing effects.

In sum, the results of this study reflect that most new teachers have three primary needs: (1) to learn basic information about the school and school system, (2) to obtain the instructional resources and adequate instructional materials to successfully carry out their assignment, and (3), to receive emotional support from colleagues and administrators.

Interestingly, results reflect that the support needs of new-to-system teachers are virtually the same as the support needs of beginning teachers. Although beginning teachers will generally need more help with classroom management, both groups of experienced teachers will need help in the three primary areas. It is important, then, that all teachers in a state of transition receive induction support.

So we see that socialization processes are important because they affect the general satisfaction of teachers and their feelings of autonomy and self-worth. These factors, in turn, are important because general satisfaction consistently relates to decreased turnover and absenteeism.

For more than a decade, research on teacher socialization has found that new teachers are often left to sink or swim. This study and many others like it clearly suggest that this practice is no longer defensible (Huling-Austin L., 1987; Wanous, 1980; Friebus, 1977; Zeichner, 1983; Van Maanen, 1979). Many teachers undergo dramatic changes as they move from school to school and find that the norms, beliefs, and values are different from those with which they are familiar. How teachers are helped to deal with the changes they encounter in an unfamiliar school organization can make a difference in their levels of satisfaction and can ultimately determine whether they remain in the organization or in teaching.

Since 15% of new teachers leave the profession after the first year, teacher induction and orientation programs have the potential to increase the retention rate of promising teachers. One way to begin to encourage individuals who enter teaching to remain may be to investigate the processes by which school organizations socialize their newcomers. Certainly, early experiences in the school setting play a major role in determining teacher effectiveness and career commitment.

This topic is also important because of its relationship to effective teaching and because of concerns about the aging of the current teaching force, the number of beginning teachers who leave the profession within the first five years of being employed as teachers, and growing evidence of a possible teacher shortage.

Based on the results of this study on the formal and informal socialization processes in secondary schools, the following recommendations are made:

1. School leaders and staff should consciously develop and live the norms and expectations that will make their school an effective one. All teachers who are newcomers, both beginning and experienced, should be helped to understand and learn to act in accordance with these norms and expectations so they may become an integrated member of the school organization.

2. The primary purpose of orientation should be the transmission of culture. With this in mind, then, orientation activities should provide teachers with information on the history and philosophy of the school

or district, employment benefits and procedures, the school calendar, a job description, logistical details on purchasing supplies, copying materials, and planning and conducting field trips. Information on the history of the community, its customs and values, and its expectations for its children should also be provided, as well as a list of resources used in the school.

3. Teachers in transition should not be given the least desirable teaching assignments. The number of preparations assigned to teachers in transition should also not exceed two distinct subjects.

4. Every effort should be made to assign teachers who are newcomers a room of their own with adequate supplies and equipment. This one element contributes more to the smooth transition of newcomers than any other factor, except the teaching assignment itself.

5. Teachers who are newcomers should be assigned a reduced workload during their first year in the new assignment. Released time should be granted for planning, discussions with other teachers, opportunities to observe other experienced teachers, and opportunities to develop relationships with other staff and the community.

6. All newcomers should be assigned a buddy or mentor. This individual should teach in the same department and be located close to the newcomer, if at all possible. This individual should not be assigned to evaluate the newcomer.

7. Evaluation activities should focus on informing beginning teachers about the evaluation criteria and the processes that will be used to determine when tenure is earned or advancement deserved. Teachers who are newcomers feel that two visits during the year are inadequate for evaluation and that principals should visit frequently to demonstrate support and concern.

8. Newcomers should not be assigned extra-curricular activities. In fact, extra duties should be offered to the newcomer only after the individual has spent an appreciable amount of time in the organization.

9. An administrator, supervisor, or colleague should work alongside the newcomer for at least one full day in order to answer questions pertaining to the day's activities and clarify procedures. Administrators, in particular, should provide as much support to the newcomer as possible in resolving problems.

10. Other support activities should include collegial encouragement, training in classroom management strategies and effective discipline procedures, as well as long-term professional development activities.

I hope that this study will encourage schools to implement programs specifically designed to support the special needs of beginning teachers and other new staff. I hope also that this book will serve as a useful primer for student teachers, beginning teachers, those who are returning to the profession, and any teacher who is assigned to an unfamiliar school organization.

Please remember that my intent is not to provide the reader with generalizations about all new teachers in all schools. Rather, my purpose is to provide greater understanding of the nature of the interactions and practices within a school which deeply affect new teachers and their teaching performance. These influences must be taken into account if teacher education, recruitment and retention are to become more effective processes.

And now for a moment of truth. This novel describing the experiences of the six newcomers to Melrose, in addition to being naturalistic, is also autobiographical. Five years after I entered Watson Middle School as a beginning teacher, I was promoted to assistant principal at the school. Two years later, I arrived at Melrose as principal for curriculum, instruction and staff development. As you have probably guessed, the character I represent in this novel is Cheryl Rossman.

My description of how I was socialized at Watson Middle school is true. The events described occurred exactly as they were written. My first year was traumatic, but certainly not as traumatic as Gail's.

After having prepared for a career in teaching, my desire to teach was almost as strong as my desire to be a journalist. I was determined to succeed. But by the end of my first year, I knew something had to change.

It was at the beginning of my second year that I began to use an approach very similar to the one Don DeLoach uses in an attempt to create teachable moments. I found that because students are allowed to participate in the formulation of classroom rules and procedures they develop feelings of ownership that work to curtail their interest in breaking rules. What happens, in effect, is that students police themselves and teachers can spend their time teaching.

The one surprise this study held for me was that students served as the teachers' primary socializing agents. They served as constant sources of information and affirmation. It was through the teachers' day-to-day interactions with students that the culture of the school was made manifest. So I feel I have come full circle. I no longer have to wonder how I learned the ropes at Watson Middle or how other teachers who enter unfamiliar school organizations manage. Students are very powerful sources of information and assistance.

Finally, this novel is not an indictment against Melrose Comprehensive High School. As the novel reflects, efforts were made to provide induction support to the newcomers. An orientation session and a tour were conducted, attempts were made to ensure that newcomers had adequate materials, and several colleagues and administrators did reach out to Gail on several occasions. My point is that the Melrose staff did more than some schools are currently doing.

That's not to say that Melrose was doing enough. Melrose was not. Hopefully, newcomers to Melrose are receiving more assistance and attention, especially from the administration. Principals are now able to assign newcomers a buddy or mentor, and instructional coaches are available to work with teachers on a daily basis. Hopefully, the next Gail Simmons who walks through those doors will not leave prematurely.

And so I ask you, school practitioners, what support will you provide for your next Gail Simmons? I hope those of you who are currently working in schools can say with confidence that you will be prepared for your next Gail Simmons. Use this novel as inspiration to do more for newcomers to your schools.

To all student teachers, you can become the effective teacher you want to become. Believe you can and work hard at it. Teaching is hard work, but the rewards are worth your efforts. Seek out those teachers who serve as your role models and spend time with them now so you will know what to expect when you face your first classroom of challenging students.

If you are already in your first, second, or third year of teaching, I offer you my hearty congratulations! Consider yourself fortunate. You will touch more lives than anyone in any other profession. What an opportunity! Take your responsibility seriously, but do have fun. And no, you don't have to wait until Christmas.

APPENDICES

APPENDIX A

STUDENTS' EXPECTATIONS OF THEIR TEACHERS

STUDENTS' EXPECTATIONS OF
THEIR TEACHERS

1. To have control of the class.

2. To be flexible but strict.

3. To make learning interesting and fun.

4. To demonstrate that they are organized, on the ball, and know what is going on.

5. To establish rules and boundaries, as well as consequences for breaking the rules.

6. To care about student learning.

7. To give students respect.

8. To treat students fairly.

9. To exhibit a positive attitude and friendliness.

10. To act human rather than holy.

APPENDIX B

HOW STUDENTS DETERMINE WHEN TO GIVE A TEACHER A HARD TIME

How Students Determine When to Give a Teacher a Hard Time

1. When a teacher says get quiet and everyone keeps talking.

2. When a teacher loses your work.

3. When a teacher reports to class late and is out of the classroom frequently.

4. When a teacher sits at his or her desk most of the time.

5. When a teacher's classroom stays dirty.

6. When a teacher displays a negative attitude.

7. When a teacher is too nice and fails to establish rules and boundaries.

8. When a teacher has too many rules.

9. When a teacher ignores disruptive behaviors.

10. When a teacher doesn't treat students fairly.

APPENDIX C

THE NOVEL METHOD

THE NOVEL METHOD

Purpose of the Study

The purpose of this study was to investigate the formal and informal processes through which teachers who were newcomers to a selected high school were socialized to the existing norms and expectations. The following questions guided the study:

1. How do new teachers acquire information on the norms, values, and beliefs of the school organization?

2. How do new teachers determine and satisfy the organizations expectations?

3. How do new teachers strive to adapt to the new culture?

4. How do new teachers fulfill their needs for acceptance, achievement and affiliation?

5. In what ways does the actual teaching experience in a school differ from teachers' expectations?

6. How can school organizations ease the transition as teachers move from newcomers to accepted members of the school community?

Theoretical Framework

Organizational socialization theory provides the primary framework for this study which investigated the process through which new teachers acquire the information, knowledge and skills necessary to become an accepted member of the school organization to which they are assigned. The major focus of this study was on the socialization of teachers to the norms and expectations of a given school.

This study attempts to determine the socialization practices in which public school organizations engage and looks at both the processes and outcomes of socialization. From some perspectives, social and organizational structures determine socialization outcomes and the individual is defined as relatively passive in adapting to structural factors (Wentworth, 1980). This study views the socialization processes as interactive. Although individuals are viewed as social products shaped by the expectations and actions of significant others, they are seen as capable of initiating action and reflexive thought (Scarr-Salapatek, 1973; Brieschke, 1981).

The socialization of teachers takes place through interaction with others, both formally and informally (Chafetz, 1976). Thus, within an organizational setting, the development of professional roles and attitudes is related to the meanings that result from social interaction and the interpretive processes employed by individuals. In accordance with this interactive perspective, emphasis is on describing the teachers' socialization experiences to determine how they learn the ropes and who serves as their socializing agents. In accordance with the organizational socialization perspective, this study focuses on the question: How do teachers learn the norms, values, and beliefs which allow them to function as effective members of the school organization?

Approached from an anthropological perspective, this study incorporates theories of transition derived from <u>Rites of Passage</u> (1960) in an effort to broaden our understanding of the socialization processes teachers typically experience in school organizations. From this perspective, new teachers are viewed as those making a transition. New teachers are viewed as those making a transition from status of pupil to that of teacher as well as those making the transition from old-timer to newcomer.

The study is not limited to new teachers who are making the passage from the status of pupil to that of teacher, but includes those who are making the passage from full-time careers in business and industry or who are reporting to a new teaching assignment at a different school. My hunch is that the passage is not easy in any case and that school practitioners can do much to influence the nature of this period of transition.

In summary, this study draws principles from three theoretical strands in an attempt to determine what happens to teachers as newcomers in school organizations. Grounded in organizational socialization theory, symbolic interaction theory, and in transition theory, the study takes a comprehensive look at newcomers to school organizations as it relates the teacher socialization process to the field of anthropology. These theories and fields of study do not provide answers to the research problem in question. But they do provide illumination to the topic and frames of reference through which this problem is to be approached.

Significance of the Study

Even though we know what problems plague beginning teachers, we still know little about the person-specific and situation-specific nature of these problems (Veenman, 1984). This study delineates the kinds of problems and their relationships to the characteristics of the type of school and classroom. This study provides much needed information on the features of educational situations that are problematic, about the meanings underlying these situations, and about the significant personal characteristics of teachers who interact with these situations. This research based on an interactive paradigm which takes into account person-environment interactions, might provide this much-needed information (Hunt, 1975; Mangusson, 1981).

This study looked at beginning and experienced teachers in a given school and the socialization processes that affected them during their transition. Since socialization is interactive, this research examined not only the formal and informal socialization practices but also investigated the dynamics between individual teachers and a particular school organization. Study results contribute to the body of knowledge relating to teacher socialization and hold significance for the recruitment and retention of teachers.

Limitations of the Study

This field study extends our knowledge of teacher socialization and describes the processes in a large comprehensive high school. Since the sample size was small and the case study participants came from a specific high school, application to newcomers to other schools cannot be assumed. Similarities in the structure and orientation of high schools do exist, but variations in school operation and induction systems remain. The results are not intended, therefore, to be construed as broadly representative of all high school teachers.

The Research Site

The research site selected was a suburban high school in the southeastern United States. The large, comprehensive high school was composed of 1,700 students and 100 teachers. The school also employed four full-time guidance counselors, one executive principal and five assistant principals. The selected site was not unlike other suburban high schools in the district except in terms of the predominant population being African-American. The SES of the student population was also not unlike that of other high schools in the district.

Sample Selection

Teachers working in high schools in a selected metropolitan school district for the first time served as the target population for this study. The twelve newcomers to the research site were representative of the total population of newcomers in the school district on the basis of the three categories of new teachers under investigation.

As was the case at the research site, the teachers in the district who were newcomers to their schools fell into three distinct categories. Fifty percent (50%) were new to the building, twenty-five percent (25%) were new to the system, and twenty-five percent (25%) were beginning teachers. Teachers new to the building were familiar to the school district by virtue of the fact that they had taught in another school in the area. Because they had been transferred either voluntarily or by administrative request in order to meet the changing instructional demands of the various schools, they were newcomers to the school to which they were currently assigned. Teachers new to the system were experienced employees from other school districts or former teachers who had renewed their certificates and returned to teaching after a long period of absence. Newcomers falling into the beginning teacher category were first-year teachers having had no formal teaching experience.

Six newcomers at the research site were new to the building, three were new to the system, and three were beginning teachers. Thus, the largest population of newcomers was experienced teachers transferring from other schools in the district.

In order to select participants for the study, the researcher held a meeting with the twelve newcomers at the selected site during their first days on the job. The purpose of the meeting was to make the newcomers aware of the nature and objectives of the research and to provide an explanation of the approximate amount of time the study would entail.

A questionnaire developed especially for this study was given to each member in attendance. The questionnaire seeking demographic and attitudinal data, gathered information relating to the personal, educational and experiential backgrounds of the new teachers. Sections of the questionnaire also related to career commitment and levels of satisfaction with their choices of occupation.

It was made clear that only those individuals who voluntarily returned the questionnaire would be included in the final selection process. The teachers were also told that members who elected not to return the questionnaire would receive no further communication regarding the research study and would suffer no penalty.

The primary selection criterion was that each participant be a full-time beginning or experienced teacher working in the research site for the first time. No particular age range was established for participation, and gender and ethnicity were not important variables. The researcher hoped to obtain an equal number of beginning and experienced participants for comparison purposes.

The six subjects who returned their questionnaires indicating their willingness to participate included three beginning and three experienced teachers. The researcher met with the six subjects to officially notify them of their selection for the study and to answer any questions pertaining to the research procedures and objectives. Each participant was then asked to read and sign the consent forms.

Subjects were assured that participation was voluntary, that they could withdraw their participation at any time, and that no information from the study would become part of any personnel file or evaluation.

Choice of Research Methodology

The research method chosen was a field study approach using multiple data sources and qualitative analysis. In order to examine the individual and organizational factors that contributed to the teachers' socialization experiences, intensive case studies of the six teachers were developed over a period of one year. Structured and unstructured interviews, surveys, questionnaires, observations, and individual diaries were used to collect data from the seven teachers who were newcomers to the school. In an effort to conduct a comparative analysis of the effects of previous experience on the teachers' socialization, three of the subjects were veteran teachers with a minimum of five years of experience and three of the subjects were beginning teachers.

The categories, hypotheses, and theoretical statements described in this study are grounded in qualitative data drawn from the intensive case studies of the six high school teachers. Using the qualitative means of data collection allowed this researcher to go beyond the surface impressions and get into the in-depth culture of the organization. Although a number of questions related to the teachers' experience were addressed in this study, the impact of personal and organizational influences on the teachers' socialization was studied in each case. Taken together, the case studies provide an abundance of data useful to the development of grounded theory.

Reliability and Validity Checks

A system designed to validate the data derived from the intensive case studies also served to establish some degree of reliability. The major professor charged with overseeing the project, Terrence E. Deal, judiciously scheduled group interviews with the subjects at the beginning, middle and end of this study. He played an active role in the conduct of these sessions by serving as a devil's advocate as well as assisting in the identification of emerging themes. The high level of trust established between Dr. Deal and the subjects encouraged the sharing of information that the participants may have withheld from the researcher.

The group interview held at the end of the study was a particularly powerful one. Subjects openly shared their impressions of the nature of their socialization and offered some suggestions for change. All conclusions drawn in this study are corroborated by the subjects themselves. In addition, a random sample of each of the subjects' students was surveyed and the total population of teachers in the school system who were new to secondary schools was surveyed to determine if their experiences were comparable to that of the six participants.

Data Collection

Data for this study were collected during the 1987-1988 academic year and employed participant observation as the major data collection strategy. Participant observation is not a single methodology, however, but a research strategy which combines several methods in order to reach a desired end (McCall and Simmons, 1969; Gall, Gall, & Borg, 1983).

The blend of methods and techniques which were used for discovering the processes by which the teachers who were newcomers learned the ropes in the organization were respondent interviewing, direct and indirect observation, direct participation, questionnaires, surveys and diaries.

This blend of methods, also referred to as triangulation, increased the richness and depth of the data collected and allowed this researcher to more fully understand the motives, interests, and perceptions of the newcomers. This investigator was able to produce an analytic description of the experienced and beginning teachers which provided a means for testing the hypothesis that transition theory is a useful prototype for understanding the teacher socialization processes existing in schools. The participant observation strategy also allowed the researcher to go beyond the surface impressions and investigate the culture of the organization.

Respondent Interviewing

The primary data collection strategy used was respondent interviewing, supplemented by direct and indirect observation. An interview guide was developed based on the research questions in this study. Several interview questions were derived from the interviews developed by Lortie (1975).

Formal interviews with respondents were conducted after their first few weeks on the job, after four months, at the seventh month and at the end of the year. Formal interviews were used to actively control interaction along lines bearing upon the research. The participants engaged in active conversation, stemming from the general, specific, and provocative questions posed by the researcher. The researcher made a special effort to probe for the meaning of events and experiences. Informal interviews or conversations were held as situations would permit. The researcher took advantage of opportunities to hold casual conversations because of their potential for yielding a broader context for more effective formal interviewing (Shatzman and Strauss, 1973).

Formal interviews lasted for approximately fifty minutes and were scheduled at mutually agreeable times. The investigator began the initial formal interview by requesting a career sketch and then proceeded to more specific probes related to career choice and philosophy of teaching. Although an interview guide was used, this investigator allowed the content of each interview to give more form and substance to the subsequent one. The investigator also probed for more specific data stemming from information gathered from other respondents that appeared to reflect a pattern. As each situation dictated, a particular posture was assumed in posing questions; incorporating the devil's advocate questions, hypothetical questions, focusing on the ideal, and testing propositions and interpretations which seemed to be emerging. Consent from each respondent to audio-tape the interviews so that note-taking would not be necessary was secured.

A group interview was held at the middle and end of the year to provide an opportunity for distinguishing between shared and variable perspectives and for substantiating findings and major themes. These validation sessions were joint meetings conducted by this researcher and the major professor charged with overseeing the research project. A series of six interviews were conducted periodically with teachers in the research setting (total interview hours = 36). The interviews, which were transcribed, yielded approximately 900 single-spaced pages of data. Interview data were collected and coded openly, without theoretical control, to produce categories relevant to the teacher socialization problem under investigation.

Direct Observation

Throughout the data collection process, the researcher capitalized upon past experience as an index to interpreting what she heard and witnessed. This strategy was particularly helpful in interpreting direct and indirect observation data. Direct observations were pre-scheduled with each subject and were called shadowing periods. Subjects were shadowed while in the process of carrying out their duties for two full days.

Attention was focused on the subjects dress, general deportment, interactions, the physical setting, noise level, engaged time, disengaged time, vigor of engagement, discussions, interruptions, and whether they worked alone or in collaboration with other teachers. During the direct observations, the researcher remained as unobtrusive as possible in an effort to avoid contaminating the data (Gall, Gall & Borg, 1983).

Indirect Observations

Indirect observations were used to supplement direct observations. These indirect observations were obtained from informants who were on the scene during the researchers' absence. Informants were department heads, colleagues, assistant principals, and students. The informants provided leads to follow, information on generally known rules, and observed incidents which the researcher was unable to observe. Since the researcher could not be at all places at all times, the informants increased the investigator's accessibility to information. Informal conversations with informants served to double-check the validity of accounts received from the subjects.

Invaluable information was gained from students of the subjects who engaged in informal conversations regarding their perception of the extent to which participants were adapting to the culture of the school. Similar conversations were held with assistant principals, colleagues, and department chairpersons.

Various other data were collected unobtrusively as the investigator took an active part in the relevant activities in which the subjects were engaged. These activities included faculty meetings, department meetings, faculty socials, pep rallies, assemblies, athletic events and PTSA meetings. By doing so, the researcher received the same socialization as ordinary members, acquired similar perspectives, and encountered similar experiences. In this way, the researcher acquired some sense of the subjective side of events which could be less readily inferred if observed without taking part. A log was kept of comments heard, colleagues with whom subjects appeared to be spending time, and questions subjects asked of various members of the organization.

Survey Data Collection

Surveys comprised the second phase of this study. This phase of the study was designed to validate and expand the scope of the data derived from the intensive case studies. The surveys were developed and administered to the target population and to students.

The total population of teachers in the school system who were new to secondary schools were surveyed to determine if their experiences differed from the six teachers who were studied up close. Of the 101 teachers surveyed, sixty-six responded. Eighteen respondents (28%) were beginning teachers and forty-eight respondents (72%) were veteran teachers. This survey was mailed to the 101 teachers at the end of the 1987-88 school year and sought information regarding the nature of their socialization experiences in the schools and the influence of various socializing agents. Although some of the information obtained was demographic, most of the questions were open-ended so that respondents would not be lead to respond in certain ways and would be required to elaborate on their responses.

The student surveys were administered to groups of randomly selected students enrolled in the participants' classes. The surveys, which were administered during the last few weeks of the school year, proved to be more economical than interviewing and also served to protect the anonymity of the students. The students (N=365) were surveyed only with the consent of each teacher participating in the study. Questions used in the survey were derived from theories and impressions gleaned from interviews with the subjects, informal conversations with their students, and observations of day-to-day events. The student surveys proved to be an important means of following-up on leads and substantiating data obtained from the subjects.

Diaries

After the initial interview, each subject was asked to maintain a diary of their daily experiences, reactions, and sentiments. Each subject was supplied with a stenographer's pad which was to be used for the diary entries. Each page was subdivided in a fashion whereby respondents could record frustrations on one side and encouragements on the other. The diaries provided additional information on the daily experiences of the respondents and served to validate the interview data. One of the respondents who submitted a very detailed diary felt that this strategy forced her to evaluate daily occurrences and helped her to resolve emergent conflict more effectively.

Data Analysis

Data were collected and analyzed according to qualitative research guidelines and according to specific guidelines for grounded theory research and constant comparative analysis. This approach to qualitative research begins with questions rather than hypotheses. Data are produced and examined through an inductive process designed to generate theory. The research procedures used allowed categories to emerge directly from the data and earn their way into the developing model.

Approximately 300 hours were spent collecting data in the school setting. Major categories were developed from line-by-line examination of interview data. Follow-up data collection procedures were employed in the form of surveys to check the validity of data generated by the interviews. Observations were conducted throughout the research process.

Immediately following an interview or observation, this researcher would retreat to an isolated area and develop a set of field notes. The field notes were comprised of descriptions of observations, reactions, and meanings derived from the experience. These observational, methodological, and theoretical notes were developed as a means of recording units of pertinent information which could be retrieved for analysis at a later date. Page numbers and dates were judiciously recorded on all field notes and tapes (Shatzmann and Strauss, 1973).

In order to record pertinent information collected from observations, this investigator made use of a sampling graph which listed the various settings, events, and individuals that she was likely to encounter while conducting observations. The pertinent variables were listed under each category and checked on each occasion when an incident relating to a particular variable was witnessed. The sampling graph represented a frequency distribution at the end of the study.

The survey data were tabulated and analyzed in relation to findings of previous research on teacher socialization. Previous research studies cited in the literature review and the theoretical framework guided the classification of interview data. Final categorization of data followed patterns identified through careful study of interview responses and common experiences. Multiple evidence from the surveys, interviews and observations supports all assertions and recommendations.

APPENDIX D

THE FLASHBACK

THE FLASHBACK

This researcher's comprehensive review of the existing literature on the socialization of teachers as newcomers spanned a two year period. It began with a careful reading of two classical pieces: The Sociology of Teaching (Waller, 1932) and Schoolteacher: A sociological study (Lortie, 1975). These works were most revealing and instructive. Although I was offended by many of Waller's interpretations of teachers' status, Lortie's work confirmed that the teaching occupation has changed very little in the last four decades. I was equally as captivated by the richness of Lortie's descriptions and by the appropriateness of the questions he posed in his Five Towns' interviews for his study.

Once the two classical works were read, I reviewed the large body of research on the problems of beginning teachers and the changes which they typically undergo during their first year. A review of two broad categories of research, the outcomes of socialization and the influences on the process, lead to an investigation of when the socialization process actually begins.

The impact of school cultures on the socialization process was then reviewed as I began to focus on schools as organizations. My purpose was to determine the extent to which the socialization process in schools matches the process in other organizations.

School Organizations and Teacher Socialization

A review of the various modes and stages of organizational socialization gave meaning to the experiences of teachers in schools and allowed me to narrow my focus to the consideration of individual teachers and specific schools. Here I begin with Waller.

Waller addressed the issue of what school organizations do to teachers. Using the ethnographic research methods, Waller analyzed situations teachers routinely encountered to determine the characteristic effects these situations produced.

He described teaching as an occupation that routinely restricted the intellectual and emotional development of its employees through strict community norms governing teacher behavior and through more subtle psychological and social pressures characteristic of the teaching role itself. Waller discovered that these influences determined teachers' behaviors, to a great degree, and contributed significantly to their socialization.

Since Waller's work, research on teacher socialization has focused almost exclusively on beginning teachers. A review of these studies indicates that beginning teachers encounter problems such as classroom discipline (Lagana, 1970; McDonald and Elias, 1983), student motivation (Adams and Martray, 1980), apathetic parents (McIntosh, 1977), and meeting individual student needs (Blasé, 1980; Nias, 1984).

The research further suggests that such problems tend to produce shifts in beginning teachers toward authoritarianism in their attitudes toward pupils (Day, 1959; Lagana, 1970), custodialism in their attitudes toward pupil control (Hoy, 1968; McArthur, 1978; Morrison and McIntyre, 1967), and realism (Adams, 1982; Blasé, 1982; Chafetz, 1976; Lortie, 1975; Weinberg, 1975). Although we know what problems plagued beginning teachers, we still know little about the person-specific and situation-specific nature of these problems.

Other studies have provided valuable data regarding changes in teachers provoked by job-related variables. For example, Haller (1967) found evidence of decreased language complexity in experienced primary and elementary school teachers. Becker (1952) demonstrated that the social-class characteristics of students have an important effect on the attitudes, behaviors, and career patterns of teachers. Cusick (1983) tied the development of teacher classroom style to concerns about student control and discipline. McNeil (1983) found that social studies teachers presented content in objectified formats and omitted complex content in response to low levels of student motivation.

Although these and other studies have contributed to our knowledge about specific aspects of the socialization process, no published research comprehensively describes, from both the beginning and experienced teachers' perspective, the range of personal and organizational factors precipitating changes in teacher attitude and behavior over time and the meaning of such factors for teachers.

Crase (1979) defines the teacher socialization process as one wherein an individual learns, unlearns and adjusts new and old behaviors so that one's performance is commensurate with the school's expectations. Researchers also refer to this process as unfreezing (Wanous, 1980). Additionally, researchers view induction programs as socialization for beginning teachers (Schlechty, 1985; Galvez-Hjornevik, 1986; Brooks, 1986, 1987; Dunifon, 1985; Huling-Austin, 1985, 1986, 1987; The Holmes Group, 1986; Odell 1986, 1987, 1988).

Induction has been defined as a planned, organized orientation procedure (Ashburn, 1987; Egan, 1981); as the implantation of school standards and norms so deeply within the teacher that the teacher's behavior spontaneously reflects those norms (Schlechty, 1985); and, as the first step in staff development (Hall, 1982).

Teacher socialization, then, includes not only the formal training one receives to acquire the skills to become a teacher, but encompasses the formal orientation period one experiences when the teacher first arrives at the school. Because the period immediately after entry is an important period of adjustment and adaptation for both beginning and experienced teachers, its effects on both groups should receive a wider range of treatment in the literature.

The literature reflects two broad categories of research on teacher socialization: research assessing socialization outcomes and research attempting to determine the factors influencing socialization. Although researchers agree on the outcomes of teacher socialization, research focusing on the factors which influence the socialization process reflects wide disagreement.

Much of the research has focused on the nature of teachers' university training as the primary factor influencing the socialization process, citing the inadequacy of college courses to prepare students for the challenges they face (Giroux, 1980; Popkewitz, 1976, 1979; Battersby, 1983; Pruitt, Lee & Marion, 1978; Bullough, 1987; Bush, 1987; Crow, 1987).

Other research has pointed to the school bureaucracy as the primary factor influencing socialization, as new teachers are faced with the conflicting demands of school organizations (Becker, 1951; Eddy, 1969; Helsel and Krchniak, 1972; Hoy and Rees, 1977; Driscoll, 1983; Bird & Little, 1986). Another group of researchers have examined the influence of role models on the socialization of beginning teachers, claiming teachers pattern their teaching style after previous models (Leslie, Swiren and Flexner, 1977; Lortie, 1975; Pataniczek and Isaacson, 1981; Galvez-Hjornevik, 1986; Gerhke, 1984; Blasé, 1985).

Recently, researchers have begun to assess the impact of certain structural, personal, and internal influences on teacher socialization. These researchers claim that teachers develop theories, beliefs and certain classroom behaviors as a result of their work. The assertion is that it is not the students or other personal agents who affect the teacher most, but the structural nature of the classroom and its working conditions.

The structural frames within which teaching takes place, such as time, resources, curriculum, textbooks, number of students, and ability levels of students, are viewed as more important influences (Jordell, 1987; Clark & Peterson 1986; Veenman, 1984; Houston, 1988; Howey, 1989).

The research with respect to the outcomes of teacher socialization is consistent throughout the literature. Researchers have found that the progressive and liberal views students adopt during college shift after their initial teaching experience (Zeichner & Tabachnick, 1981) and that new teachers adopt traditional values and attitudes toward education in order to work within the bureaucracy (Becker, 1951; Eddy, 1969; Rothstein, 1979).

Early studies used specially formulated questionnaires such as the Minnesota Teacher Attitude Inventory (MTAI) and Pupil Control Ideology (PCI) to determine the impact of socialization on beginning teachers' attitudes toward teaching. These studies reflect that beginning teachers tend to feel that they possess less knowledge about teaching at the end than at the beginning of the first year (Gaede, 1978); to shift from progressive to more conventional teaching practices (Hanson & Herrington, 1976); and to rate themselves as less happy and optimistic at the end of the first year than at the beginning (Wright & Tuska, 1968). While these early studies point to shifts in perspectives, they fail to identify specific factors involved in the socialization process.

Research conducted by Hoy and Rees (1977) focused on the school bureaucracy and how it changes the attitudes and values of individuals once they are hired to teach. They found that student teachers became more bureaucratic in orientation and more custodial in their pupil control orientation after a nine week student teaching experience in secondary schools. From these survey results, Hoy and Rees (1977) concluded that there are some important changes in orientation during initial teaching experiences, although the basic beliefs of students are not modified during a nine week period.

Additionally, researchers do not agree on exactly when formal socialization begins. Issacson (1981), for instance, argues that formal socialization into the teaching profession begins with university training programs before the student receives certification. Isaacson claims that by requiring students to take courses which inadequately prepare them for the classroom, universities leave them with few options but to conform to existing methods of instruction, which are usually the same methods they observed during their childhood.

Lortie (1975) suggests that the psychological isolation of students in education programs initiates the socialization process. Students proceed through most education programs and internships on an individual basis. Lortie claims the absence of a "shared ordeal" in teacher education is the appropriate socialization for teachers, as they will be entering into an organizational system in which the members are isolated. Lortie also alludes to the limits of teacher socialization, describing the experience as largely self-socialization where one's own orientation stands at the core of becoming a teacher. Essentially, Lortie feels socialization patterns in teaching affect many aspects of the occupation, such as teacher status, self-esteem, and conservatism.

Several researchers view the socialization of teachers as highly context specific, relating the process to the merger of persons who possess varying levels of skills and capabilities and various individual histories with school contexts which differ in the constraints and norms they present to the new teacher (Ryan, 1970; Tisher, 1982; Murphy & Huling-Austin, 1987; Rosenholtz, et al., 1986).

Many studies depict teachers as being so totally overpowered by the school organization that conformity to established norms and practices is their only option, short of leaving the organization. New teachers are described as being unable to resist pressures to conform to norms for teacher behavior and so vulnerable that they are easily transformed into shapes acceptable to their particular schools (Hanson & Herrington, 1976; Lacey, 1977; Pellegrin, 1976; Ryan, et al., 1980).

Despite the existence of such empirical evidence which would support this view and which demonstrates the vulnerability of beginning teachers to the press of institutional forces, studies also exist which demonstrate the resilience and firmness of beginning teachers to pressures to change (Zeichner & Tabachnick, 1983; Nias, 1984). Many have challenged the commonly accepted view that the socializing influence of the workplace is conservative in comparison to the university's influence (Bartholomew, 1976; Giroux, 1980; Zeichner & Tabachnick, 1981).

Several studies demonstrate that certain attitudes of teachers appear to be resistant to change; such as their perceptions of self in the teaching role, their evaluation of teaching as an occupational activity and their vocational interests and aspirations (Power, 1981; Petty & Hogben, 1980; Mardle & Walker, 1980). Others call into question the notion of reality shock, but see anticipatory socialization as the most significant influence on teacher development (Mardle & Walker, 1980; Goodlad, 1982; Rauth & Bowers, 1986). Mardle and Walker (1980) capture the essence of this view when they claim that pre-service experience may be more influential than college training or the colleague-control of later years, since teachers do not become re-socialized during their college training nor in the classroom.

Both groups of studies, those that document changes and those which do not, demonstrate the fact that some teachers experienced significant shifts in attitudes while others did not. Among those teachers who changed, the changes were often in different directions.

Admittedly, when attention is focused on the socialization of individual teachers, neither group of studies is very helpful in illuminating how specific teachers are socialized in particular settings. We are almost never given specific information in these studies about the personal characteristics and life histories of the teachers or detailed information about the settings in which they work. On the one hand, new teachers are seen as prisoners of the past, yielding to the influence of anticipatory socialization or pre-service training, and on the other hand they are seen as prisoners of the present, yielding to the institutional pressures emanating from the workplace. It is significant that in neither case are new teachers viewed as making any substantial contribution to the quality or strength of their own socialization.

The writer would like to suggest, through this novel, that conformity to the past or present is not the only outcome of teacher socialization; and that even when conformity does occur, it occurs in different degrees, in different forms, has different meanings for different individual teachers and within different organizational contexts.

Although most studies have looked at the influence of university training, the school bureaucracy, and role models on the outcomes of teacher socialization, few studies have examined how one's own culture interacts with the culture of the school organization to influence to a greater extent the outcomes of socialization. Thus, it is important to look at the culture of organizations in order to understand its impact on the socialization process.

The Culture of Organizations

The concept of culture has been defined in many ways. It has been defined as the way things are done (Bower, 1966); as observed behavioral regularities (Goffman, 1959, 1967; Van Maanen, 1979); as the norms that evolve in working groups (Homans, 1950); as the dominant values espoused by an organization (Deal & Kennedy, 1982); as the philosophy that guides an organization's policy toward employees and customers (Ouchi, 1981; Pascale, et al., 1981; Peters & Waterman, 1982); as the rules of the game for getting along in the organization or the ropes that a newcomer must learn in order to become an accepted member (Schein, 1968, 1978; Van Maanen, 1976, 1979; Ritti & Funkhouser, 1982); as the feeling or climate that is conveyed in an organization by the physical layout and the way in which members interact with each other and with outsiders (Tagiuri & Litwin, 1968).

Cultural patterns have been conceptually and empirically linked to performance, morale, image, job satisfaction and commitment. Many researchers suggest that job satisfaction and commitment to an organization are a direct result of accomplishing the right match between the needs of the individual and the capacity of the organization to reinforce those needs (Dean, 1981, 1983, 1984).

Deal and Kennedy (1982) describe schools as complex organizations representing a culture which must be learned by all members of the group. Building a strong supportive culture in public schools has far reaching implications for the future of public education in terms of recruitment, maintaining talented teachers, and obtaining adequate financial support at a time when resources are dwindling and families with school-aged children are decreasing (Task Force on Teaching as a Profession, 1986; National Commission on Excellence in Education, 1983; Darling-Hammond, 1984, 1987; Schlechty, 1984, 1985).

Researchers have looked at differences in socialization outcomes in terms of school traditions and cultures and have discovered that, under some conditions, teachers were able to maintain a perspective which was in conflict with the dominant institutional cultures in their schools (Zeichner & Tabachnick, 1983; Metz, 1978; Hammersley, 1977). One possible explanation offered for this pattern was that school cultures were often diverse and that various subcultures attempt to influence new teachers in contradictory ways. Zeichner & Tabachnick (1983) found that contradictions within the school culture, particularly contradictions between the formal and informal school cultures, played a significant role in enabling the teachers to successfully implement a method of teaching which was very different from that which went on around them.

Researchers have argued that the school culture into which neophytes are socialized is homogeneous (Hoy, 1968; Gibson, 1976; Schwille, 1979). Indications are that school cultures are apparently not always diverse and contradictory within any one setting, but when they are, the contradictions seem to provide room for new teachers to implement a "deviant" pedagogy, or at least to establish individual expressions of teaching (Feiman-Nemser, et al., 1986; Grant, 1985, 1987). Nevertheless, it seems clear that new teachers give some direction to the strength and quality of their own socialization whether in schools with homogeneous or diverse cultures.

Lacey's (1977) concept of social strategy which researchers have used to understand the degree to which teachers conform to organizational demands obviously has application here (Zeichner & Tabachnick, 1983). The three social strategies Lacy identified were internalized adjustment, strategic compliance, and strategic redefinition.

Internalized adjustment occurs when the individual complies with the constraints and believes the constraints of the situation are for the best. Strategic compliance is when the individual complies with the authority figure's definition of the situation but retains private reservations about them. And, lastly, strategic redefinition of the situation implies that change is brought about by individuals who do not possess the formal power to do so. They achieve change by causing or enabling those with formal power to change their interpretation of what is happening in the situation.

Obviously, the ways in which new members are taught the correct way to perceive, think, and feel in relation to problems differ from organization to organization. If we accept the premise that the various strategies organizations use to socialize new members have different effects, then looking at the processes of organizational socialization becomes an activity of paramount importance.

Organizational Socialization

While enrolled in a course in organizational theory I found that this process of learning the ropes, of discovering what to do, how to perform, and what is important in a school is known as organizational socialization. At the same time, I learned that schools as organizations are considered to be loosely coupled (Weick, 1976). Thus, my purpose for reviewing the literature on organizational socialization was to determine how closely teachers' experiences in schools match the classical organizational socialization process.

Organizational socialization captures the essence of what newcomers experience when they enter an unfamiliar organization or assume a new role within an organization with which they are familiar. Some major contributors to this field are Merton (1957, Schein (1978), Van Maanen (1977), Feldman (1976), and Wanous (1980).

Reality shock is the term coined by Hughes (1958) to characterize what newcomers often experience when entering unfamiliar organizations. During this time the newcomer is inundated with unfamiliar cues. It may not be clear to the newcomer just what constitutes a cue, let alone what the cues mean. In other words, there is no gradual exposure and no way to confront the situation a little at a time. Reality shock among teachers has been well documented in the literature (Dean, 1984; Gaede, 1978; Huling-Austin, 1987).

The definitions of teacher socialization which appear in the literature correspond with the organizational perspective. Organizational socialization is defined as the process by which employees are transformed from outsiders to participating and effective insiders (Feldman, 1976), the process by which new members are taught to adapt to an existing organizational culture and learn their individual roles within it (Schein, 1978; Wanous, 1980), and, as the process by which an individual learns the values, norms, and acceptable behaviors which permit one to function as a member of an organization (Dean, 1983; Van Maanen, 1976; Jablen, 1982, 1984; Louis, 1980; Weiss, 1978; Wilson, 1984).

Research on organizational socialization has focused primarily on long-range outcomes of the process such as commitment (Steers, 1977), satisfaction (Feldman, 1976; Katz, 1978), and performance (Berlew & Hall, 1966; Wanous, 1977).

Researchers agree that organizational socialization can play a major part in ensuring that the newcomer encounters early success experiences, feels comfortable with his or her role, and develops a high level of commitment to the organization. One occupation which has drawn national attention recently due to indications of low levels of employee commitment, satisfaction and performance is teaching. Consequently, many who are committed to finding long-range, workable solutions to the problems in school organizations are convinced that attention needs to be directed toward an analysis of school work cultures (Deal, 1983, 1984, 1985, 1986; Snyder, 1988; Lambert, 1988; Little, 1982).

Pfeffer (1981) points out that organizations can be viewed as systems of shared meanings and that one key task of managers is the building and maintenance of those systems, those shared paradigms, shared languages, and shared cultures. Much administrative work involves using language, symbolism and ritual to develop shared meanings and beliefs in organizations. Management, therefore, means developing a consensus of beliefs and a shared construction of social realities in organizations. Ceremonies and talk are essential tools for projecting the symbols, values and rationalizations that function to reduce conflict, increase productivity, and create an image.

There is little disagreement with the concept that in order for teachers to become fully socialized they must learn their individual roles within the new school culture as well as discover the values, norms, and acceptable behaviors which permit them to be considered insiders or members of the organization. Thus, conceptualization of the socialization process tends to be universal throughout the literature. Yet, descriptions of the process in schools and in other organizations show wide variation.

A number of different modes of socialization appear in the literature, which suggest that organizations use a variety of ways to socialize new members. Literature on the stages of socialization that newcomers typically undergo and the modes of socialization that various organizations use will be reviewed in order to draw some tentative conclusions about the nature of the socialization occurring in schools.

The various stages of socialization newcomers typically undergo appear in the literature as models of socialization depicting a three-stage process (Buchanan, 1974; Porter, Lawler & Hackman, 1975; Van Maanen, 1975; Feldman, 1976; Schein, 1978; Wanous, 1980). A model recently proposed by Feldman (1981) includes an anticipatory socialization stage, encounter stage, and a change and acquisition stage.

The first stage, anticipatory socialization (Merton, 1957; Feldman, 1976), encompasses all the learning that occurs before a new member joins an organization. This stage is illustrated in the university training as well as in the influence of previous role models. Individuals aspiring to teach generally experience a shorter period of formal anticipatory socialization than their counterparts who are attracted to the established professions. The two years of professional training for teachers is much shorter than the four to eight years required in medicine or law and has low impact on teacher trainees. Unlike other occupations, however, those who decide to enter the teaching field have had exceptional opportunity to observe members of the occupation at work. It can be said that teacher socialization begins for all candidates during childhood since they spend years assessing and observing teachers at work. In most occupations today, the work is not open to public scrutiny. Unfortunately, the observations youngsters make prior to becoming teachers cause many to underestimate the difficulties of teaching (Lortie, 1975).

The extensive period of observation results in teaching candidates entering college classes with very strong assumptions about the conduct of their chosen occupation. Yet newcomers entering other occupations are more likely to feel that their information and knowledge of the craft is limited. Because of this unique feature, teacher training is considered to be almost intuitive. The mind of the education student, in contrast to the engineering or medical student, is not a blank page (Lortie, 1975; Becker, 1961).

Thus, the aggregate of college courses do not create a dramatic change in outlook. Of major importance in the anticipatory socialization of teachers is that the extensive period of observation they experience during their childhood acquaints students with the tasks of the teacher and fosters the development of orientations toward work, but it does not lay the foundation for informed assessments of teaching technique or analytic orientations toward teachers' work (Lortie, 1975).

According to researchers, unless teacher trainees undergo training experiences which will offset their individualistic and traditional experiences, the occupation will be staffed by people who have little concern with building a shared technical culture (Houston, 1988; Jensen, 1987; National Commission on Excellence, 1983; Roth, 1981). In the absence of such culture, the diverse experiences of teachers will play a vital role in their day-to-day activity. In this respect, the extensive period of observation promotes continuity and traditionalism rather than change.

The anticipatory socialization stage, which occurs prior to entry and usually includes the interview, comprises only a small segment of this study of new teachers. This study focuses primarily on the encounter stage, when the individual passes from outsider and enters the organization to begin work. Experiences during the encounter stage are said to shape the newcomer's future orientation to the organization.

During the encounter stage, newcomers' expectations are tested against the realities of the workplace. The second stage, encounter (Porter et al., 1975; Van Maanen, 1975), is the period when the new recruit enters the organization and seeks what the organization is really like. The individual enters the organization and is introduced to the values and expectations the system holds. It is at this point at which some initial shifting of values, attitudes, and skills is likely to occur. The shifting of values, attitudes and skills appears to be minimal for those who teach.

Most schools start the formal socialization process of teachers with an orientation period. During orientation, the teachers learn what rules they are to follow, and become acquainted with the hierarchy of the organization. Teachers learn the patterns or behavior expected and become acquainted with the school's culture. Studies reflect that teachers are expected to follow routine lesson plans and are instructed as to what types of materials they are to have in their classrooms. Teachers are judged on their formal lesson plan, the beauty of their classrooms, and their ability to control students (Eddy, 1969; Becker, 1951; Helsel & Krchniak, 1972).

It is in the third stage, change and acquisition (Porter et. al., 1975) that relatively long-lasting changes take place during the typical organizational socialization process. New members master the skills required of their jobs, successfully perform their new roles, and make some satisfactory adjustment to their work group's values and norms. The encounter stage typically precedes the change and acquisition stage, yet there is evidence that these two stages overlap. Because teachers work in isolation, they maintain many of the values and orientations they possess at entry. The literature suggests that teachers are generally self-directed and very selective in the skills they choose for mastery.

The aggregate of these data reflect that socialization occurs primarily through the internalization of teaching models during the many years students spend in close contact with teachers, from elementary school through college (Leslie, Swiren and Flexner, 1977; Lortie, 1975; Pataniczek and Isaacson, 1981; Pruitt, Lee and Marion, 1978). The basic conclusion drawn by these researchers is that teachers teach as they were taught.

Although it is assumed that newcomers to organizations experience each of the socialization stages at some point regardless of their occupation, the strategies organizations use to teach new members the correct way to perceive, think, and feel in relation to the problems encountered at the various stages differ from organization to organization. A variety of organizational socialization strategies appear in the literature. Of those mentioned, five pure types seem to emerge. These are described as (1) training, (2) education, (3) apprenticeship, (4) debasement experiences, and (5) cooptation or seduction (Schein, 1968; Van Maanen, 1979; Wanous, 1980; Katz, 1980).

Training refers to the acquisition of skills and/or knowledge related to one's job performance. Training in most organizations is done on either a full or part-time basis and may be termed training-while-working or working-while-training, depending upon whether the organization's emphasis at post entry is on work or training. The emphasis in public school organizations, of course, is on work. Teachers who seek further training typically return to colleges and universities because school systems rarely provide training for its members (Wanous, 1980; Schein, 1979).

The second socialization strategy, education, involves informing newcomers of the various policies, procedures and norms of the organization. This education is sometimes combined with skill training or provided with no focus on actual job skills. Though not always provided, the education strategy in public school organizations focuses around the policies, procedures, and practices of the school as opposed to job skills.

A third socialization strategy, apprenticeship, usually contains equal elements of both training and education. This involves a one-on-one relationship between the newcomer and an insider who has the responsibility both to train and educate the newcomer. The formal apprenticeship for prospective teachers involves the placement of the trainee with a veteran teacher for a six to eight week period of practice teaching.

The fourth socialization strategy described in the literature is termed debasement experiences because of the organization's attempts to unfreeze the newcomer from previously held beliefs and values, and to humble the person so that a new self-image can be developed by the organization. Two types of debasement experiences appear in the literature: sink-or-swim and the upending experience (Schein, 1968; Wanous, 1980; Van Maanen, 1979).

The sink-or-swim ploy is designed to humble the newcomer by assigning a job to be done, but then giving very little definition to the task or the amount of authority the newcomer has, and giving little support. The upending experience is designed to alter the newcomer's expectations and self-image by putting the newcomer in a situation in which early failure is guaranteed or giving the newcomer some very menial responsibilities. In either case, the newcomer's confidence is shaken so that the organization is in a better position to exert influence. The typical sink-or-swim strategy in public school organizations has more than likely caused many new teachers to change occupations. New teachers are often assigned very basic classes, oversized classes, or multiple preparations which are difficult to handle.

The fifth and final socialization strategy discussed in the literature is a subtle attempt at cooptation or seduction. Cooptation is described as a process where the newcomer is admitted to the organization and then is abruptly absorbed into it. In public schools, the neophyte is held responsible for the full range of teaching tasks from the very first day of employment. The purpose of the seduction process is to present the newcomer with a number of tempting choices. The illusion of a choice is maintained, but in fact one alternative is more attractive than the other.

It appears that a mix of the three of the socialization strategies described in the literature is employed in public school organizations during the encounter stage. These are education, sink-or-swim debasement experiences and cooptation. The education phase of socialization may occur as a formal orientation process designed by the administration, or it may occur through the newcomer's informal interactions with colleagues who will supply information on the way we do things around here. Both the sink-or-swim and cooptation debasement experiences typify the manner in which teachers are thrust into classrooms during the initial encounter stage with little information and limited assistance. Training and apprenticeship typically occur during a prospective teacher's college experience at the anticipatory socialization stage.

The mode of socialization which most accurately depicts the events beginning teachers experience is sink-or-swim debasement. From the very first day, the beginning teacher is held responsible for the full range of teaching tasks. No distinction is made between the work requirements of a beginning teacher and a veteran. Aside from this, little assistance or information is received from the administration.

Although few organizations employ all of these strategies, the result an organization seeks in using certain modes of socialization is to cause the newcomer to develop a commitment to the organization and change some basic attitudes and beliefs. The literature reflects that the various strategies organizations use to socialize newcomers do have different effects. Although the modes of socialization ascribed to by various organizations are similarly defined, the nature and effects of the various modes are quite different; particularly when comparing the nature of socialization in educational organizations with that existing in other organizations.

Because of their isolation, beginning teachers frequently work things out as best they can before asking for help. The result of this pervasive isolation from peers is that teaching tends to become an individual rather than collegial enterprise. The gaps in collegiality are matched by weaknesses in the subculture of classroom teachers. Although there are indications that peers influence newcomers, there is little to suggest that this amounts to significant sharing of common understandings and techniques.

One central theme stood out in Lortie's (1975) conversations with teachers regarding the influence of peers. Teachers insisted that they adopt the ideas of peers on a highly selective basis. In Lortie's study (1975) teachers qualified statements on what they had learned from other teachers and were clearly reluctant to present themselves as initiating colleagues.

Aside from this, teachers lack a technical core of knowledge or practice upon which they can base decisions or develop techniques. Lortie (1975) reminds us that teaching is not like crafts and professions whose members talk in a language specific to them and their work. Thus, the absence of a common technical vocabulary limits a beginner's ability to tap into an existing body of practical knowledge. Without such a framework, the neophyte is less capable of understanding the classroom realities. Beginning teachers must laboriously construct their own reality by devising ways of perceiving and interpreting what is significant based upon their individual judgments. Norms reflect a reliance on self rather than others and personally held rather than authoritative opinions. Doctors, lawyers, and engineers have the benefit of authoritative sources resulting from the codification and documentation of past successes.

Dreeben (1970) points out that teachers, as opposed to other professionals, are easily influenced by their clients because they do not have access to a highly developed technology. Dreeben feels that the absence of a technical core of knowledge weakens teachers' authority so that they must base their activity on their personal skills and abilities. Jordell (1987) mentions the high degree of affect that teachers develop with their clients.

The position that students are important agents in the socialization of teachers is well documented in the literature (Lortie, 1975; Friebus, 1977; Zeichner, 1983; Dreeben, 1979). It is one of the main positions taken by Lortie as he cites students as teachers' main source of psychic rewards. Friebus (1977) found that students play a major role in the legitimization of student teachers, and in their experiences of success and failure. Zeichner (1983) refers to a couple of studies which show that students are important because it is the students, more than the colleagues, who validate the teacher's efforts.

Thus the stages typical in classical forms of socialization differ for teachers. The teaching occupation continues to be characterized by individualism where any possible addition to their repertoires is based strictly on personal preferences. Since education, training and work experience do not seem to fundamentally change individual predispositions toward teaching, Lortie (1975) feels that socialization into teaching is primarily self-socialization in that teachers' personal predispositions remain highly relevant throughout the teaching career.

In organizations where no formal socialization processes exist, then, the attitudes, values, and orientations individuals bring with them continue to influence their work. This appears to be the case in public school organizations.

This review of the literature on teacher socialization, then, points to a need for more research in the area. For instance, Chafetz (1976) recommended further research on the patterns which give beginners support and on the kinds of teachers who survive and persevere in their attempts to meet students' needs. Lichtenstein (1980) proposed studying the socialization experiences of a large sample of new teachers to discover if findings are characteristic of beginning teachers.

A study of the improvement of beginning teachers' work environments in order to maximize beginning teacher performance was recommended by Cable (1981). Further exploration of ways to improve teacher preparation programs and in-service for new teachers was proposed by Gatewood (1986). Finally, Coleman (1986) saw a need for qualitative research studies which employ intensive interviews to provide additional information on the supervisory assistance available to beginning teachers.

In summary, the research on teacher socialization covers a wide range of topics dealing with the problems of beginning teachers and student teachers. Research on the problems experienced teachers encounter when they report to an unfamiliar school organization is limited, just as is research on the socialization process at specific schools.

REFERENCES

Adams, R. D., Hutchinson, S., & Martray, C. (1980). *A developmental study of teacher concerns across time.* Paper presented at the Annual Meeting of the AERS, Boston, Mass.

Adams, R. D., & Martray, C. (1981). *Teacher development: A study of factors related to teacher concerns for pre, beginning, and experienced teachers.* Paper presented at the Annual Meeting of the AERS, Los Angeles, CA.

Blasé, J. J., & Greenfield, W. (1982). On the meaning of being a high school teacher: the beginning years. *High School Journal 65*: 263-271.

Ashburn, E. A. (1987), (Winter). Current developments in teacher induction programs. *Action In Teacher Education*, 8 (4), 41-44.

Bartholomew, J. (1976). Schooling teachers: The myth of the liberal college. In G. Whitty & J. Young (Eds.), *Explorations in the politics of school knowledge.* Duffield, England: Nofferton Books.

Battersby, D. & Ramsay, P. (1983). Professional socialization of teachers: Towards improved methodology. *New Education*, 5 (1), 11-86.

Becker, H. S., (1951). The career of the Chicago public schoolteacher. *American Journal of Sociology*, 57, 470-477.

Becker, H. S., Greer, B., Hughes, E. & Strauss, A. (1961). *Boys in white: Student culture in medical school.* Chicago: University of Chicago Press.

Becker, H. S. (1952). Social class variations in the teacher-pupil relationship. *Journal of Educational Sociology* 25: 451-465.

Berlew, D. E., & Hall, D. T. (1966). The socialization of managers: Effects of Expectations on performance. *Administrative Science Quaterly, 11,* 207-223.

Bird, T., & Little, J. W. (1986). How schools organize the teaching occupation. *Elementary School Journal, 86* (4), 493-511.

Blasé, J. J. (1980). *On the meaning of being a teacher: A study of the teacher's perspective.* Doctoral dissertation, Syracuse University, Syracuse New York.

Blasé, J. J., & Greenfield, W. (1982). On the meaning of being a high school teacher: The beginning years. *High School Journal 65:* 263-271.

Blasé, J. J. (1985, October). The socialization of teachers: An ethnographic study of factors contributing to the rationalization of the teacher's instructional perspective. *Urban Education, 20* (3), 234-256.

Blasé, J. J. (1986, April). Socialization as humanization: One side of becoming a teacher. *Sociology of Education, 59* (2), 100-113).

Bower, M. (1966). *The will to manage.* New York: McGraw Hill.

Brieschke, P. (1981, April). *Teacher careers: Decoding the organization.* Paper presented at the Annual Meeting of the American Educational Research Association, Los Angeles, CA.

Brim, O., & Wheeler, S. (1966). *Socialization after childhood: Two essays.* New York: John Wiley & Sons.

Briscoe, F. G. (1976). *The professional concerns of first year secondary teachers in selected Michigan public schools: A pilot study.* Unpublished doctoral dissertation, Michigan State University.

Brooks, D. M. (1986). *Programmatic teacher induction: A model for new teacher professional development.* Project Description prepared for the Richardson Independent School District's New Teacher Induction Program, Richardson, TX.

Brooks, D. M. (Ed.) (1987). Teacher induction: A new beginning. *Papers from the National Comission on the Education Process.* Reston, VA: Association of Teacher Educators.

Buchanan, B. (1974). Building organizational commitment: The socialization of managers in work organizations. *Administrative Science Quarterly, 19,*533-546.

Bullough, R.V., Jr. (1987). Accommodation and tension: Teachers, teacher role. and the culture of teaching. In J. Smith (Ed.), *Educating teachers: changing the nature of pedagogical knowledge,* (pp. 83-94). London: The Palmer Press.

Bush, R. N. (1987). Teacher education reform: Lessons for the past half century. *Journal of Teacher Education. 38* (3), 13-19.

Chafetz, M. M. (1976). The socialization of two beginning elementary teachers. (Doctoral Dissertation, Syracuse University, 1977). *Dissertation Abstracts International. 38,* 2441A.

Chatman, R. M., & Deal, T. E. (1989 Spring). Learning the ropes alone: Socializing new teachers. *Action in Education, 11* (1), 21-29.

Clark. C. M., & Peterson, P. L. (1986). Teacher's thought processes. In M.C. Wittrock (Ed.), *Handbook of research on teaching,* 3rd. ed. (pp. 255-96). New York: Macmillan.

Cooper, C.C. (1988). Implications of the absence of black teachers: Administrators on black youth. *The Journal of Negro Education, 57* (2), 123-124.

Crase, D. (1979). Socialization of secondary school teachers. *Physical Educator, 36,* 9-13.

Crow, N. (1987). *Socialization within a teacher education program: A case study.* Unpublished Doctoral dissertation, University of Utah, Salt Lake City, Utah.

Cusick, P. A. (1983). *The egalitarian ideal and the American high school: Studies of three schools.* New York: Longman.

Darling-Hammond, L. (1987). *Beyond the commission repots: The coming crisis in teaching.* Santa Monica, CA.: Rand Corporation.

Day, H. P. (1959). Attitude changes of beginning teachers after initial teaching experience. *Journal of Teacher Education, 10,* 325-328.

Deal, T. E., & Kennedy, A. A. (1982). *Corporate cultures.* Reading, MA.: Addison-Wesley.

Deal, T. E. (1983, March). High schools without students: Some thoughts on the future. *Phi Delta Kappan, 64* (7), 485-491.

Deal, T. E. (1984, Fall). Educational change: Revival tent, tinkertoys, jungle, or carnival? *Teachers College Record, 86* (1), 124-137.

Deal, T. E. (1985, February). National commissions: Blueprints for remodeling or Ceremonies for revitalizing public schools. *Education and Urban Society, 17* (2), 145-156.

Deal, T. E. (1986, January). Deeper culture: Mucking, muddling, and metaphors. *Training and Development Journal, 40* (1), 32.

Dean, R. A. (1983). Reality shock, organizational commitment, and behavior: A realistic job preview experiment. *Dissertation Abstracts International, 42,* 12A, 5226. University Microfilms No. 8s-12, 381.

Dean, R. A. (1983). Reality shock: The link between socialization and organizational commitment. *Journal of Management Development, 2,* 55-63.

Dean, R. A. (1984). *Reality shock: A predictor of the organizational commitment of professionals.* Research Monograph. Lexington, Virginia: School of Commerce, Economics, and Politics, Washington and Lee University.

Dreeben, R. (1970). *The nature of teaching.* Glenview, IL: Scott Foreman.

Dreeben, R. (1973). The school as a workplace. In R.M.W. Travers (Ed.), *Second handbook of research on teaching.* Chicago, IL: Rand McNally.

Driscoll, A. (1983, October). *The socialization of teachers: Career rewards and levels of professional concern.* Paper presented at the Annual Meeting of the Northern Rocky Mountain Educational Research Association, Jackson Hole, WY.

Dunifon, W. S. (1985). *Excellence in secondary education: The induction of teachers: Career rewards and levels of professional concern.* Paper presented at the Secondary Education Conference Excellence Week, Normal, IL.

Eddy, E. M. (1969). *Becoming a teacher.* New York: Columbia University, Teachers College Press.

Egan, K. (1981). *Beginnings: The orientation of new teachers.* Washington, D. C.: National Catholic Educational Association.

Feiman-Nemser, S., & Floden, R.E. (1986). The cultures of teaching. In M.C. Whittrock (Ed.), *Handbook of research on teaching.* (3rd. ed.) (pp. 505-526). N.Y.: MacMillan.

Feldman, D. C. (1976). A practical program for employee socialization. *Organizational Dynamics, 57* (2), 64-80.

Feldman, D. C. (1976). A contingency theory of socialization. *Administrative Science Quarterly, 21* (4), 433-452.

Feldman, D. C. (1981). The multiple socialization of organization members. *Academy of Management Review, 6* (2), 309-318.

Fiske, E. B. (1987, May). Teaching teachers examined critically. *The Sunday Courier.* (Evansville, IN.), B1.

Friebus, R. J. (1977, May-June). Agents of socialization involved in student teaching. *Journal of Educational Research, 70*(5), 263-268.

Fuchs, E. (1967). *Teachers talk: Views from inside city schools.* Garden City, New York: Doubleday.

Gaede, O. F. (1978). Reality shock: A problem among first-year teachers. *Clearinghouse, 51,* 405-409.

Gall, Gall & Borg (1983). Educational Research: An Introduction. San Fracisco, CA: Pearson, Inc.

Galvez-Hjornevik, C., & Smith, J. J. (1986). Support teaching in beginning teacher programs. *Journal of Staff Development, 7* (11), 110-122.

Gerhke, N. J. & Kay, R. S. (1984). The socialization of beginning teachers through mentor-protégé relationships. *Journal of Teacher Education, 35* (3), 21-24.

Gibson, R. (1976). The effects of school practice: The development of student perspectives. *British Journal of Teacher Education, 2,* 241-250.

Giroux, H. (1980). Teacher education and the ideology of social control. *Journal of Education, 162,* 5-27.

Goffman, E. (1967). *Interaction Ritual.* New York: Doubleday.

Goffman, E. (1959). *The presentation of self in everyday life.* New York: Doubleday.

Grant, C. A., & Sleeter, C. E. (1985). Who determines teacher work: The teacher, the organization, or both? *Teaching and Teacher Education, 1,* 209-220.

Grant, C. A., & Sleeter, C. E. (1987). Who determines teacher work: The debate continues. *Teaching and Teacher Education, 3* (1), 61-64.

Haller, E. J. (1967). Pupil influence in teacher socialization: A socio-linguistic study. *Sociology of Education, 40,* 316-333.

Hall, G. E. (1982, May-June). Induction: The missing link. *Journal of Teacher Education, 33* (3), 53-55.

Hall, G. E., & Jones, H. L. (1976). *Competency-based education.* Englewood Cliffs, New Jersey: Prentice-Hall.

Hammersley, M. (1977). *The social location of teacher perspectives.* Milton Keynes, England: The Open University Press.

Hanson, D., & Herrington, M. (1976). *From college to classroom: The probation year*. London: Routledge & Kegan Paul.

Helsel, A., & Krchniak, S. (1977). Socialization in a heteronomous profession: Public school teaching. *Journal of Educational Research, 66*, 89-93.

Holmes Group. (1986). *Tomorrow's teachers: A report of the Holmes Group*. East Lansing, Michigan: Michigan State University College of Education.

Homans, G. (1950). *The human group*. New York: Harcourt Brace Jovanovich.

Houston, W. R. (Ed.), (1988). *Mirrors of excellence: Reflections for teacher education from training programs in ten corporations and agencies*. Reston, VA: Association of Teacher Educators

Howey, K. R. (1969). *Profiles of preservice teacher education: Inquiry into the nature of programs*. Albany: State University of New York Press.

Hoy, W. K. (1969). Pupil control ideology and organizational socialization: A A further examination of the influence of experience on the beginning teacher. *School Review, 77*, 257-265.

Hoy, W. K. (1968). The influence of experience on the beginning teacher. *School Review, 76*, 312-323.

Hoy, W., & Ress, R. (1977). The bureaucratic socialization of student teachers. *Journal of Teacher Education, 28*, 23-26.

Hudson, L. Grissmer, D., & Kirby, S. (1991). *New and returning teachers in Indiana: The role of the beginning teacher internship program*. Sana Monica, CA: Rand.

Hughes, E. C. (1958). *Men and their work*. New York: Free Press.

Hulin-Austin, L., Barnes, S., & Smith, J. J. (1985). *A research-based staff development program for beginning teachers*. Austin: University of Texas,

Research and Development Center for Teacher Education. (ERIC Document Reproduction Service No. Ed. 261-989).

Hulin-Austin, L. (1986). What can and cannot reasonably be expected from teacher induction programs. *Journal of Teacher Education, 37* (1), 2-5.

Hulin-Austin, L. (1987). Teacher induction. In D. M. Brooks, (Ed.), *Teacher induction: A new beginning* (pp. 3-24). Reston VA: Association of Teacher Educators.

Hunt, D. E. (1975). Person-environment interaction: A challenge found wanting before it was tried. *Review of Educational Research, 45,* 209-230. Issacson, N. (1981). *Secondary teachers' perceptions of personal and organizational support during induction to teaching.* Eugene: University of Oregon.

Jablin, F. M. (1982). Organizational communication: An assimilation approach. In M. E. Roloff & C. R. Berger (Eds.), *Social cognition and communication* (pp. 255-286). Beverly Hills: Sage Publisher.

Jablin, F. M. (1984). *The assimilation of new members into organizational communication systems: A longitudinal investigation.* Paper presented at the Annual Convention of the International Communication Association, San Francisco.

Jensen, M. C. (1987). *How to recruit, select, induct, and retain the very best teachers.* ERIC Clearinghouse on Educational Management, Eugene, Oregon.

Jones, J. (1986, October). The disappearing teacher. *Tennessee Teacher, 54*(3), 7-9.

Jordell, K. O. (1987). Structural and personal influences in the socialization of beginning teachers. *Teaching and Teacher Education, 3* (3), 165-177.

Katz, D., & Kahn, R. (1978). *The social psychology of organizations* (2nd ed.). New York: John Wiley & Sons.

Katz, R. (1980). Time and work: Toward an integrative perspective. In B. M. Staw (Ed.), *Research in Organizational Behavior* (vol. 2, pp 81-127). Greenwich, CT.: JAI Press.

Lacey, C. (1977). *The socialization of teachers*. London: Methuen and Co., Ltd.

Ladson-Billings, Gloria (2001) *Crossing over to Canaan: The journey of new teachers in diverse classrooms*. San Francisco: Jossey-Bass.

Lambert, L. G. (1988, March). Building school culture: An open letter to principals. *NASSP Bulletin, 72* (506), 54-62.

Lagana, J. (1970). *What happens to the attitudes of beginning teachers?* Danville, Illinois: Interstate Printers.

Little, J. W. (1982, Fall). Norms of collegiality and experimentation: Workplace conditions of school success. *American Educational Research Journal, 19* (3), 325-340.

Lortie, D. C. (1975). *Schoolteacher: A sociological study*. Chicago: University of Chicago Press.

Louis, M. (1980). Organizations as culture bearing milieu. In Louis Pondy, et al., (Eds.), *Organizational symbolism*. Chicago: University of Chicago Press.

Louis, M. (1980, June). Surprise and sensemaking: What newcomers experience in entering unfamiliar organizational settings. *Administrative Science Quarterly, 25*, 226-251.

Magnusson, D. (Ed.). (1981). *Toward a psychology of situations: An interactional perspective*. Hillsdale, NJ: Eribaum.

Martle, G., & Walker, M. (1980). Strategies and structure: Critical notes on teacher socialization. In P. Woods (Ed.), *Teacher strategies: Explorations in the sociology of the school*. London: Croom Helm.

McArthur, J. M. (1978). What does teaching do to teachers? *Educational Administration Quarterly, 14*, 89-103.

McCall, G., & Simmons, J. (1969). *Issues in participant observation.* New York: Random House.

McDonald, F., & Elias, P. (1983). *The transition into teaching: The problems of beginning teachers and programs to solve them.* (Summary Report No. 141). Educational Testing Services, Princeton, NJ.

McIntosh, J. G. (1977). The first year of experience: Influence on beginning teachers. *Dissertation Abstracts International, 38*: 3192-3193.

McNeil, L. M. (1983). *Defensive teaching and classroom control.* Washington, D.C.: National Institute of Education.

Merton, R., Reader, G., & Kendall, P. (Eds.), (1957), *The student physician.* Cambridge, MADS: Harvard University Press.

Metz, M. (1978). *Classrooms and corridors.* Berkley, CA: University of California Press.

Mitchell, M., & Chisholm, I. (1977). Practice helping the first-year-out teachers. *The Educational Magazine, 34,* 33-35.

Morrison, A., & McIntyre, D. (1967). Changes in opinions about education during The first year of teaching. *British Journal of Social and Clinical Psychology, 6,* 161-163.

Murphy, S., & Huling-Austin, L. (1987, April). *The impact of context on the classroom lives of beginning teachers.* Paper presented at the Annual Meeting of the American Educational Research Association, Washington, D.C.

National Commission on Excellence in Education. (1983). *A nation at risk: The imperative for school reform.* Washington, D.C.: Author.

Nias, J. (1984). *A more distant drummer: Teacher development as the development of self.* Cambridge, England: Cambridge Institute of Education.

Odell, S. J. (1986, January-February). Induction support of new teachers: A Functional approach. *Journal of Teacher Education, 37* (1), 26-29.

Odell, S. J. (1987). Teacher induction: Rationale and critical issues. In D.M. Brooks (Ed.), *Teacher induction: A new beginning* (pp. 69-80). Reston, VA: Association of Teacher Educators.

Odell, S. J. (1988, February). *Characteristics of beginning teachers in induction context*. Paper presented at the Annual Meeting of the American Associa- tion of Colleges for Teacher Education, New Orleans, LA.

Ouchi, W. G. (1981). *Theory Z*. Reading MASS: Addison-Wesley.

Palmer, Parker J. (2007). *The courage to teach*. San Francisco, CA: John Wiley & Sons.

Pascale, R., & Athos, A. (1981). *The art of Japanese management*. New York: Simon & Schuster.

Pataniczek, D., & Isaacson, N. (1981). The relationship of socialization and the concerns of beginning secondary teachers. *Journal of Teacher Education, 32*, 14-17.

Pellegrin, R. (1976). Schools as work settings. In R. Dubin (Ed.), *Handbook of work, organization, and society*. Chicago: Rand McNally.

Peters, T. J., & Waterman, R. H., Jr. (1982). *In search of excellence: Lessons from America's best-run companies*. New York: Harper & Row.

Petty, M., & Hogben, D. (1980). Explorations of semantic space with beginning Teachers: A study of socialization into teaching. *British Journal of Teacher Education, 6*, 51-61.

Pfeiffer, J. (1981). Management as symbolic action. In L. L. Cummings & B. M. Staw (Eds.), *Research in organizational behavior* (Vol. 3). Greenwich, CONN: JAI Press.

Popkewitz, T. S. (1976, April). *Teacher education as a process of socialization: The social distribution of knowledge*. Paper presented at AERS Convention, San Francisco, CA.

Popkewitz, T., Tabachnick, B., & Zelchner, K. (1979). Dulling the senses: Research in teacher education. *Journal of Teacher Education, 30*, 52-60.

Porter, L. W., & Hackman, J. R. (1975). *Behavior in organizations.* New York: McGraw-Hill.

Power, P. G. (1981). Aspects of the transition from education student to beginning teacher. Austrialian *Journal of Education, 25,* 288-296.

Pruitt, K., & Lee, J. (1978). Hidden handcuffs in teacher education. *Journal of Teacher Education, 29,* 69-72.

Rauth, M., & Bowers, G. (1986). Reactions to induction articles. *Journal of Teacher Education, 37,* (1), 38-41.

Ritti, R., & Funkhouser, G. (1982). *The ropes to skip and the ropes to know.* Columbus, OH: Grid.

Rosenholtz, S., Bassler, O., & Hoover-Dempsey, K. (1986). Organizational conditions of teacher learning. *Teaching and Teacher Education. 2* (2), 91-104.

Roth, R. A. (1981). Trainers in business and industry: Implications for colleges of education. *Journal of Teacher Education, 32* (2), 33-34.

Rothstein, S. W. (1979). Orientations: First impressions in an urban junior high school. *Urban Education, 14,* 91-116.

Ryan, K. (1970). *Don't smile until Christmas.* Chicago: University of Chicago Press.

Ryan, K., Newman, K, Mager, G., Applegate, J., Lasley, T., Flora, R., & Johnston, J. (1980). *Biting the apple: Accounts of first year teachers.* NY: Longman.

Scarr-Salapatek, S., & Salapatek, P. (1973). *Socialization.* Columbus, OH: Charles E. Merrill.

Schatman, L., & Strauss, A. (1973). *Field research.* Inglewood, Cliffs, NJ: Prentice-Hall.

Schein, E. H. (1978). *Career dynamics: Matching individual and organizational needs.* Reading, MASS: Addison-Wesley.

Schein, E. H. (1968). Organizational socialization. *Industrial Management Review, 2,* 37-45.

Schein, E. H. (1971). The individual, the organization, and the career: A conceptual scheme. *Journal of Applied Behavioral Science, 7,* 401-426.

Schein, V. E. (1979, April). Examining an illusion: The role of deceptive be- haviors in organizations. *Human Relations, 32* (4), 287-295.

Schlechty, P. C. (1985). A framework for evaluating induction into teaching. *Journal of Teacher Education. 36* (1), 37-41.

Schlechty, P. C., & Joslin, A. W. (1984, Spring-Summer). Recruiting teachers: Future prospects. *Journal of Children in Contemporary Society, 16* (3-4), 51-60.

Schlechty, P. C., & Vance, V. S. (1983). Recruitment, selection, and retention: The shape of the teaching force. *Elementary School Journal, 83* (4), 469-487.

Schwille, J. et al (1979). *Factors influencing teachers' decisions about what to teach.* East Lansing, Michigan. Institute for Research on Teaching. Research Series, No. 62.

Snyder, K. J. (1988, October). Managing a productive school culture. *NASSP Bulletin, 72* (510), 40-43.

Steers, R. M. (1977). Antecedents and outcomes of organizational commitment. *Administrative Science Quarterly, 22,* 46-56.

Tagiuri, R., & Litwin, G. (Eds.). (1968). *Organizational climate: Exploration of a concept.* Boston: Harvard Graduate School of Business, Division of Research.

Task Force on Teaching as a Profession (1986). *A nation prepared: Teachers for the 21ˢᵗ century.* New York: The Carnegie Forum on Education and the Economy.

Tisher, R. P. (1982). *Teacher induction: An international perspective on research and programs.* Australia: Monash University.

Van Gennep, A. (1960). *The rites of passage.* Chicago: University of Chicago Press.

Van Maanen, J. (1976). Breaking in: Socialization to work. In R. Dubin (Ed.), *Handbook of work, organization and society* (pp. 67-130). Chicago: Rand McNally.

Van Maanen, J. (1978). People processing: Strategies of organizational socialization. *Organizational Dynamics, 7,* 19-36.

Van Maanen, J. (1975). Police socialization. *Administrative Science Quarterly, 20,* 207-228.

Veenman, S. (1984). Perceived problems of beginning teachers. *Review of Educational Research, 54* (2), 143-178.

Waller, J. P. (1932). *The sociology of teaching.* New York: Wiley.

Wanous, J. P. (1980). *Organizational entry: Recruitment, selection and socialization of newcomers.* Addison-Wesley.

Weick, K. (1976, March). Educational organizations as loosely coupled systems. *Administrative Science Quarterly, 21,* 1-19.

Weinberg, C. (1975). *Education is a shuck:* New York: William Morrow.

Weiss, H. (1978). Social learning of work values in organizations. *Journal of Applied Psychology, 19,* 89-105.

Wentworth, W.M. (1980). *Context and understanding: An inquiry into socialization theory.* New York: Elsevier.

Wilson, C. (1984). *A communication perspective on socialization in organizations.* Paper presented at the Annual Convention of the International Communication Association, San Francisco.

Zeichner, K. M., & Tabachnick, B. R. (1981). Are the effects of university teacher education washed out by school experience? *Journal of Teacher Educa-tion, 32,* 7-11.

Zeichner, K. (1983). Individual and institutional factors related to the socialization of beginning teachers. In G. Griffin & H. Hukill (Eds.), *The first years of teaching: What are the pertinent issues?* (pp. 1-59). Austin: University of Texas, Research and Development Center for Teacher Education. (ERIC Document Reproduction Service No. ED 240 109.